Unlike her five older sisters, Miss Victoria Lynton is no beauty, but endowed instead with a lively mind and a tendency to outrageous behaviour. Bored with being a debutante in fashionable Edwardian Society and intrigued by life below stairs, she disguises herself as a nursemaid, taking a job at a grand country house in Devon.

Is it coincidence that among the house guests are Alex Beaumont, a most attractive man once glimpsed and never forgotten by Vicky, and his barrister friend, Thomas Craig? Coolly disapproving, the latter is a surprisingly frequent visitor to the nursery. How can Vicky successfully balance her subterfuge downstairs with her increasingly intriguing relationships upstairs?

GW01006178

By the same author in Masquerade

RUNAWAY MAID
THE DEVIL'S ANGEL
THE GOLDEN BRIDE
MAN FROM MONTANA

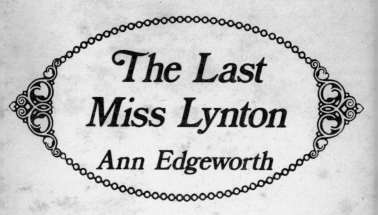

The Last Miss Lynton

Ann Edgeworth

MILLS & BOON LIMITED
London · Sydney · Toronto

First published in Great Britain 1983
by Mills & Boon Limited, 15–16 Brook's Mews,
London W1A 1DR

© Ann Edgeworth 1983
Australian copyright 1983
Philippine copyright 1983

ISBN 0 263 74243 1

The text of this publication or any part thereof may not be
reproduced or transmitted in any form or by any means,
electronic or mechanical, including photocopying, re-
cording, storage in an information retrieval system, or
otherwise, without the written permission of the
publisher.

This book is sold subject to the condition that it shall not,
by way of trade or otherwise, be lent, resold, hired out or
otherwise circulated without the prior consent of the
publisher in any form of binding or cover other than that
in which it is published and without a similar condition
including this condition being imposed on the subsequent
purchaser.

Set in 10 on 11 pt Linotron Times
04/0483

Photoset by Rowland Phototypesetting Ltd
Bury St Edmunds, Suffolk
Made and printed in Great Britain by
Cox & Wyman Ltd, Reading

CHAPTER
ONE

'So this is Victoria, the last of your brood.' The Honourable Mrs Pendred raised her lorgnette and surveyed the tall, slim, dark-haired girl who had just entered the room. 'Good heavens, she isn't even pretty!'

Her niece, Lady Lynton, twisted the rings on her fingers unhappily.

'That is not a very kind thing to say, Aunt Matilda.'

'Not kind, perhaps, but true. Your five other girls are beauties.'

'And I am not.' Vicky Lynton seated herself on a low stool near her mother. 'Perhaps Mama should have stopped at five.'

'Really, Vicky dear!' her mother protested faintly.

'How did you manage to produce such a plain piece?' her aunt demanded. Mrs Pendred was known and frequently heartily disliked for her habit of speaking frankly. 'All the other girls are pink and gold little Venuses. You've married three of 'em off well, Harriet is engaged to an American millionaire and Maud, I believe, is receiving very satisfactory attentions from that young Lord Burnley. You cannot hope to have the same luck with your last one.'

Lady Lynton was goaded into saying: 'Really, Aunt Matilda, I do not think you should speak so unfeelingly.'

'But Aunt Matilda enjoys speaking unfeelingly,' the youngest Miss Lynton said. Her eyes, an unusual and attractive silvery grey touched with green and fringed with thick dark lashes, rested on Mrs Pendred's face and the unconvincing chestnut fringe surmounted by a hat smothered in pink silk roses. 'She must keep up her reputation for saying unflattering things.'

'You are an impertinent minx!' Mrs Pendred's withered cheeks glowed under the coating of powder. 'I can only say I am sorry for your mother!'

'I wonder if you really are.' Vicky leant forward, smiling into her great-aunt's affronted eyes. 'You know, I believe you would like to have a daughter who would disagree with you and do outrageous things! It would make life interesting for you. Evelina is a most dutiful daughter—'

'But quite amazingly uninteresting.' Mrs Pendred snapped her lorgnette shut and rose, settling her feather boa around her shoulders. '*All* Henry's family were uninteresting. It is Evelina's tragedy that she did not take after me.'

'But she is a dear child and *so* amenable,' Lady Lynton protested, rising with an expensive rustle of satin. 'Must you go? Harriet and Maud will be in soon, they have gone to a matinée.'

Mrs Pendred paused on her way to the door. '*Not* that dreadful man, Shaw—or one of those *French* plays, I hope?'

'Oh no, Shakespeare,' Lady Lynton assured her hurriedly.

'It's *The Merchant of Venice*,' Vicky said as she rang the bell for the footman. 'But I wonder . . . Portia did take things into her own hands, didn't she? It might give Harriet and Maud ideas, you know.'

Mrs Pendred fixed her bright, fierce little eyes—the lorgnette was merely a fashionable accessory—on her great-niece's face and saw the mischievous light dancing in the wide, silvery eyes.

'H'm.' She began to pull on her gloves. 'It is my

opinion that *you* have a lot too many ideas, Victoria. By the way, Elizabeth,' she turned to Lady Lynton, 'why in heaven's name did you call the chit Victoria? Anything less like our late Queen I have yet to see.'

'Oh, how I agree with you, Aunt Matilda,' Vicky sighed. 'We aren't the same *shape*, for one thing. But you know, *she* couldn't often be persuaded to do what she didn't want to.'

'Vicky was very naughty and difficult about being presented,' Lady Lynton remarked, 'and she says she doesn't like doing the season. It is *so* unlike the other girls who were only too anxious to come out.'

'But they all adore balls and parties and Ascot and paying calls and I hate them,' her daughter declared vehemently. 'And I am a dreadful anti-climax after Daisy, Angelina, Flora, Harriet and Maud.'

'Nonsense, dear,' her mother said, without much conviction. 'Old Lord Durwent remarked you were a most unusual type—something about mermaids, rather odd of him I thought. And the Italian ambassador quite raved about your eyes.'

'Durwent's too old for her and the Signore has a wife *and* a mistress,' Mrs Pendred said and beckoned to Vicky. 'You can attend me to my carriage. Goodbye, Elizabeth. I shan't be in London again for at least a year; I dislike modern society. Give my love to Andrew. I suppose he's planning to visit some uncivilised country in search of bones.'

'I'm afraid so,' Lady Lynton murmured unhappily. 'The United States of America this time—and he insists I go with him.'

'It will make a nice change from bridge parties and at-homes,' her aunt said unfeelingly. 'Come, Victoria.'

'People who like me,' her great-niece observed as they left the pretty, over-furnished drawing-room, 'call me Vicky.'

Mrs Pendred sniffed. 'I disapprove of curtailing names.'

She sailed down the wide stairs in the wake of the footman, her grey silk skirts rustling and the pink roses on her hat nodding at each step she took. In the hall, she paused and pointed her ruffled parasol at a door.

'What is that room?'

'The library,' Vicky told her.

'Take me there, I want to talk to you.'

Vicky ushered her into the long book-lined room where the furniture was handsome solid mahogany and there were no small tables of bric-à-brac or chintzy chairs.

Mrs Pendred fixed her eyes on her great-niece, standing demurely before her in a leaf-green muslin dress trimmed with cream lace.

'You know how to dress, at least,' she finally pronounced. 'That muslin makes your eyes quite green. Why don't you wish to do the season? It is the dream of every girl.'

Vicky shook her head. 'I have other dreams, Aunt Matilda, and I'm afraid I don't care for fashionable society, it bores me. I agreed to be presented to please Mama, but I'm sure King Edward wasn't impressed with me. My knees stick out when I curtsey.'

Mrs Pendred gave an unexpected snort of laughter. 'Then, if you don't join the scramble to find a suitable husband, what do you propose to do, may I ask?'

Vicky glanced out of the window and saw a carriage draw up before the house.

'I'm not sure. I would like to do some sort of work, I think . . . To get away from inane dinner-parties and dances and having to go here or go there because it is the correct thing to do! Oh . . . I want to be free, Aunt Matilda!' She swung around with a smile. 'I expect you think I'm impossible.'

'You are a rebel. It must be your father's Scots ancestors, or else it's this nonsensical women's suffrage business. Heaven knows what will become of you—but if you are ever in need of help you can come to me, Vicky. Who's that in the hall?'

'Harriet and Maud have just returned.'

'I don't want to meet 'em,' Mrs Pendred said firmly, 'they treat me as if I were a hundred years old.'

'Instead of seeing you are quite young, inside—and a rebel, like me.'

'Your manners are disgraceful,' Mrs Pendred snapped, but there was a softening in the glance she turned on her great-niece. 'However, you don't simper, thank God!' She turned to the door. 'The Italian Signore was right about your eyes, they're going to get you into trouble one day.'

When she returned to the drawing-room, Vicky found her mother standing before a looking-glass tucking in a stray curl of hair and going to her, she slipped her arm around her mother's waist, a waist that was still elegant despite six daughters.

'I like Great-Aunt Matilda, Mama, she's like iced champagne, sharp and wonderfully refreshing. I've never seen her before, have I?'

'No, she seldom comes to London, she dislikes it.'

'So do I. I wonder if I take after her.'

Lady Lynton started nervously. 'Oh dear, I hope not! She has always been, well, *different*.'

'*I'm* different. Do you hate it very much that I'm not like the others, Mama?'

Her mother hesitated. 'Well, the other girls have been so easy to manage, they all thought the same.'

'They still do.' Vicky hugged her mother. 'And I have all sorts of upsetting thoughts and ideas. I make life a bit difficult, don't I?'

'I'm afraid so, dear. And now your father has this idea

of going to the United States. Not New York or Boston, but somewhere in the west where some horrid bones of prehistoric animals have been dug up! I really cannot see why he must go all that way just to look at them—and take me.'

'You should have prevented him from taking up palaeontology as a hobby,' her daughter announced. 'It's too late now. Besides, it will be very exciting.'

'I shall *not* enjoy it,' her mother sighed.

'But you will go because Father wants to have you with him. It's frightfully unfashionable of him to love his wife, but there it is, Mama, and you will have to endure it.'

'Really Vicky, you talk the greatest nonsense.' Lady Lynton turned, smiling, as Harriet and Maud came into the room. 'Did you enjoy the theatre, girls?'

Harriet, a pink and gold beauty whose large blue eyes expressed complacent satisfaction with life in general and herself in particular, tossed her gloves onto a chair.

'Oh yes, Mama, we saw a lot of people we knew.'

'Lady Grassmere was there with that handsome young guardsman,' Maud remarked, sinking into a chair. 'He seems to escort her everywhere. I wonder if—'

'He is a *great* friend of both Lady *and* Sir Ronald Grassmere,' her mother said hastily.

'Although I have yet to see him escorting Sir Ronald anywhere,' Vicky murmured thoughtfully. 'Sir Ronald is away so much that you cannot blame his wife if she chooses to—'

'*Vicky*!' her mother turned a scandalised face to her youngest daughter, 'that is quite enough! Go and tidy your hair before tea. I am expecting guests and I want you girls to help me.'

Harriet and Maud were agreeable to the idea but Vicky refused, saying she would have tea with her father who had returned from his club and who was as bored by tea-parties as she was.

He was in the library reading, having given strict orders he was not to be disturbed, when Vicky joined him.

'Now look here, Vicky,' he protested, 'why aren't you upstairs with your mother and the girls, helping to entertain your friends?'

'For the same reason you aren't,' she told him, 'and they aren't my friends. What are you reading, Father? Is it about the remains of the Tyrannosaurus Rex that have recently been discovered in the State of Montana?'

Her father put down his paper to stare at her. 'How in heaven's name do you know about that?'

'I read something about it in one of those dreary-looking papers on prehistoric discoveries which you take,' she told him, sinking into a big leather-covered armchair. 'I'm having tea with you and you can tell me how you propose to persuade Mama to accompany you when you go to America.'

Sir Andrew groaned. 'It could be a problem, Vicky. She thinks she'll be bitten by snakes or eaten by pumas or stung by scorpions. I don't believe she will come.'

'Oh yes she will, and you know it perfectly well.' She paused as the footman entered, followed by a parlour-maid, to lay a lace-edged cloth on a table and arrange the tea-tray, plate of tiny sandwiches and silver cake-basket of iced cakes. When they had left the room, she picked up the Queen Anne silver tea-pot and began to pour out tea as she asked; 'When will you go?'

'That's the greatest problem—let's have one of those sandwiches—as the society wants me to go as soon as possible while other, possibly valuable, specimens are being discovered. It is a real chance to see that extremely interesting part of the United States; heaven knows what treasures are still to be found there.' He ate his sandwich while his eyes, silvery-grey like his daughter's, gazed into a glorious future of digging up vertebrae and skulls of the great creatures that once roamed the wide and barren land.

'And of course Mama says she cannot possibly leave London while she is still chaperoning the last and least socially successful of her daughters through the season.'

'She complains that you don't want to go on with it. I must say you haven't shown much enthusiasm so far.'

Vicky leaned forward impulsively. 'Oh Father, I *don't* want to go on with it! I hate all the fuss with clothes and parties and those dreary at-homes. I find so many people dull, they're so alike and they all say the same things—I believe they *think* the same! Can't you persuade Mama to let me off the rest of the season?' She saw the gleam of hope in her father's eyes and pressed home her point. 'Harriet can go with you and Mama and spend the time with her fiancé's people in Boston, you know they want to meet her. And Maud can stay with Flora who will chaperon her and see she has plenty of opportunities of meeting Lord Burnley.'

'And what, pray, will *you* be doing?' her father asked with interest.

'Oh . . .' she tilted her head thoughtfully, avoiding her father's gaze, 'I shall visit Great-Aunt Matilda. I met her today and liked her and she has invited me to stay with her while you are away.' Truth, Vicky considered, was something to be used with discretion.

'Well, you'd be safe enough with her,' her father conceded. 'There won't be much chance in Norfolk of your getting into mischief. If things could be arranged as you've suggested—'

'They can—and they will. Mama will agree with everything if you are firm enough.'

'I am always firm enough.'

'Except with me, your favourite daughter.'

'I don't know where you got that idea,' her father grunted, but he was smiling as he reached for one of the iced cakes while Vicky slipped from the room.

As she had prophesied, Sir Andrew was perfectly capable of being firm where his passionate interest in palaeontology was concerned. His wife protested, produced reasons for remaining in London, and was finally over-ruled and resigned to setting out with her husband in two weeks' time.

'Two weeks!' she wailed to her daughters. 'Your father is *so* impatient! He never considers all that must be settled first.'

'But everything *is* settled,' Vicky assured her. 'You need not bother about anything except buying some suitable clothes for the trip.'

'I shall enjoy finishing off the season with Flora,' Maud said cheerfully, 'Archie Burnley is often at her entertainments.' Her blue eyes became misty with dreams.

'Wilbur is perfectly delighted I'm to visit his family,' Harriet announced. 'Of course it is *dreadfully* short notice, but Wilbur says Americans do everything in a rush, they like it that way.'

Despite Lady Lynton's frequent protests that all her plans were being upset and it was impossible for her to be ready in time, things proceeded smoothly, largely owing to efforts on the part of Vicky and the housekeeper. When Vicky told her mother she had written to Mrs Pendred and received an invitation to stay as long as she liked, Lady Lynton looked relieved.

'Of course *I* should really have written, but there has been so much to do. She lives in the wilds of Norfolk so you'll be safe. You must remain with her until we return. I hope it won't be very dull for you, dear.'

'Oh, I can always find ways of amusing myself,' Vicky assured her.

It was the evening of a ball being given at Devonshire House and Harriet, Maud and Vicky were to accompany their mother. Vicky had dressed early and was now standing watching Lady Lynton as she sat before her looking-glass in a pink satin dressing-jacket while her maid carefully adjusted the two pads over which Lady Lynton's hair would be arranged to give the fashionable width to her coiffure.

Sir Andrew had, for once, agreed to accompany his family, feeling he owed it to his wife who was leaving a pleasant and comfortable life for his sake. Lady Lynton was old-fashioned enough to consider it a wife's duty to obey her husband. This ball was to be the last big social event she would attend before she sailed for America and she meant to enjoy it now she need not worry about leaving her daughters. She cast a glance at her youngest daughter, slim and composed in a lilac taffeta dress, and was conscious of a feeling of relief that at least she would be spared the tiresome task of dragging an unwilling and rebellious daughter through the rigours of the rest of the London season.

Such a difficult child, she thought, but at least she could not get into any mischief with Aunt Matilda. She returned to the serious business of pulling out a strand of hair here and tucking in a wisp there, unaware that Vicky had easily followed her train of thought and was dwelling with some interest on what her mother's reaction would be—and her father's, for that matter—if they knew Mrs Pendred had never received a letter proposing a visit because it had never been written. Vicky was fond of her mother and thought it kinder to keep certain details from her. She was not quite sure what her plans were for the moment, but they did not include a visit to Great-Aunt Matilda in her big, gloomy mansion in Norfolk!

At last Lady Lynton's hair was arranged to her satis-

faction and she let the maid hook her into a charming
Worth model, a triumph of midnight-blue satin veiled in
silver lace. A spray of tuberoses fastened to the low-cut
bodice, a gauze scarf draped over her shoulders and a
feather fan completed her toilette.

'You look lovely, Mama,' Vicky exclaimed, and indeed her mother was looking her best. Much as she
deplored it, the prospect of visiting the United States
had become quite intriguing. After all, there must be
some society in the State of Montana.

The family barouche deposited them at Devonshire
House where the strip of scarlet carpet and striped
awning proclaimed entertainment within, and Lady
Lynton and her daughters made their way to a room
where they left their wraps and took a last, anxious look
at dress and hair.

The crush of guests crowding up the wide staircase
was a sign the evening was to be a success. 'The more
uncomfortable you can make people,' Vicky thought as
she squeezed past two vast matrons trailing débutante
daughters, 'the better they like it.'

She did not like it. She looked around her, seeing
faces she knew, faces she did not know, and faces she
had no desire to know, as she followed her mother and
sisters.

The ballroom was too hot and the air too heavy with
scent from the great banks of hot-house flowers and the
women's expensive perfumes. Vicky soon had partners
and was taken in to supper by old Lord Durwent who
thought her like a mermaid. She smiled and bowed,
danced and talked, letting habit take over, leaving her
mind free to wander over the possibilities open to her
once her parents had left England.

She would take a job. As a companion? A secretary to
a busy hostess? Assistant in a fashionable hat shop?
But it would be better to be out of London where she

might be recognised. She decided to visit an agency she had heard mentioned and discover what positions were open to her. Excitement swept over her as she realised she would be on her own for the first time in her life.

Of course there were problems. What if her mother wrote to Aunt Matilda? It would all need careful thinking out, but she was sure something would suggest itself to her fertile mind.

She had deceived her parents disgracefully, of course, telling lies and planning to behave in a way they would consider outrageous. Well brought up young girls obeyed their parents and the rules of society. A few who had broken away from the rigid conventions of the time were considered 'fast' and not approved of in the higher ranks of society, ranks which did not approve of a certain laxity in their King's behaviour. '*So* different from his dear mother's time,' was discreetly whispered by stern matrons.

At last the crowd thinned and Lady Lynton collected her daughters, pleased with the attentions young Archie Burnley had paid Maud which must surely lead to a proposal of marriage. Perhaps by the time she was back from America . . . but of course he would have to speak to Sir Andrew first.

Vicky, following her mother and sisters, had become separated from them by the throng of departing guests. Two men were standing just inside the door, talking. She glanced at them—and felt her step falter. The taller of the two men was extraordinarily handsome, with narrow amused eyes and a mocking mouth. She heard him say to his companion,

'No, I shan't remain in town. The Falconers have asked me to stay in Devonshire and I think I'll go. Sir Charles does one very well and has a fine stable—and an excellent cellar.'

'A bit early for the house-party round, isn't it?' his friend asked.

'But I love to break social conventions, my dear Thomas, surely you know that? Anyway, the end of the season can be dashed boring.'

'You'll meet old Lady Grange and her daughter at the Falconers'. Are you going to try your luck with the pretty little heiress, Alex?'

The tall man shook his head, smiling. 'I'm not planning to give up my freedom yet.'

With a start, Vicky realised she had been eavesdropping. She gathered her cloak around her and hurried to the carriage where her father was beckoning to her impatiently.

As they drove off she was aware of a quickened pulse and a strange feeling of excitement. She had never seen the man before, but she knew she would not forget him from that brief glimpse. Something about him, an indefinable air of self-assurance and, yes, charm, had caught and held her attention. It was quite ridiculous, of course; probably she would never see him again.

'How hot it was,' Harriet complained. 'You look quite flushed, Vicky.'

When the maid had helped her undress and had hung up the pretty lilac gown and been dismissed, Vicky went to the window and drew back the curtains. She looked out on a deserted street where shadows showed ebony-black against cold moonlight. The excitement was still with her, unexplainable and a little frightening. No man had ever affected her before like this. And she had seen him only for a few seconds. He had not noticed her, she knew, although she thought his companion had glanced at her when she paused beside them. Who was Alex—and how could she find out?

She pulled herself up sharply, annoyed that she should think like this about any man, no matter how attractive.

She went to bed determined to forget him and turn her mind to finding some work to do—and preventing her family from discovering it.

She went out next morning, ostensibly to do some shopping but with the intention of putting her name down on the agency's books. But before she had gone far, a thin drizzle of rain made her wish she had brought an umbrella. She looked around and saw a small tea-shop, very far removed from the genteel elegance of Gunters where fashionable young women were expected to take refreshment, but it was near and probably the rain would not last long.

The shop was full and she had to sit at a table already occupied by a plump, neatly-dressed girl drinking chocolate. Vicky glanced at her as she removed her gloves and recognised her as an under-housemaid once employed by her mother.

'It's Lizzie, isn't it?' she asked, smiling at the girl. 'I remember you.'

'Yes, Miss Lynton, thank you, Miss Lynton.'

'You didn't stay long with us, I think, did you?'

'Oh, I didn't leave because I wasn't satisfied, Miss. But I've always wanted to be a nurse, I'm that fond of children. Of course I knew I'd have to train as an under-nurse first, so I applied for this situation with a lady in the country.'

'And you have got it?'

'Yes, Miss. I was interviewed and the lady was kind enough to say I was the type of girl she was looking for.'

Vicky looked at Lizzie's fresh young face and neat grey coat and skirt and remembered the housekeeper had once remarked upon the girl's superior appearance and manner.

'So you are off to the country to be an under-nurse, Lizzie.'

'Well, no, Miss Lynton. You see, it's this way. Jim—

he's my intended—has had an inheritance from his auntie and he wants us to get married right away now he can start in business.' Lizzie's cheeks were pink and her eyes bright and happy. 'He won't take no for an answer, so I'm writing to Lady Falconer to say I—'

'Lady *Falconer*?' Vicky said sharply.

'Yes, Miss. Sir Charles and Lady Falconer of Wellbury Court in Devonshire. I must let the lady know I won't be coming and she'll have to find someone else.'

'She need not bother!' Vicky was sitting up very straight, her grey eyes alight with excitement. 'How extraordinary that it should be . . . Now listen to me, Lizzie.' She leaned forward. 'You are going to write to Lady Falconer to say you cannot take up the post, but you have a relation—a cousin, I think, yes, a cousin who, like you, is untrained, but whom you can most thoroughly recommend to take your place.'

Lizzie's eyes were as round as her mouth as she stared across the table.

'Someone else . . . my cousin . . . *Who*, Miss Lynton?'

Vicky sank back in her chair, laughing softly as she signalled the waitress to bring her some tea. 'Why *me*, Lizzie, of course!'

CHAPTER
TWO

BLANK surprise was succeeded by horror on Lizzie's face as she stared at Vicky.

'*You*, Miss? I—I don't understand! You can't mean you . . .'

'But I do mean it, Lizzie.' Vicky paused to pour out a cup of tea before going on. 'I have decided to take up some kind of work and I'm sure I can be a good under-nurse if I try. If you recommend me, I expect Lady Falconer will be only too glad to be saved the trouble of finding another girl and probably she won't even demand an interview if you point out how reliable I am, and willing to learn, and that I love children—and am neat and tidy in my work. Isn't that what one always says?'

'But—but I couldn't do it, Miss Lynton,' Lizzie's face was getting pinker every minute. 'Honest, I couldn't! What would your mother say?'

'My parents are going abroad for a time and are quite agreeable to my taking up some type of work.' A few more lies really can't be helped, Vicky thought, and I'm sure if Mama and Father could really understand how I feel they *would* approve. It was a comforting thought which she did not mean to examine too closely. 'I'll dictate the letter for you and you can send it right away. We'll go to a stationers for some writing paper.'

'Oh, Miss Lynton, I couldn't do it, indeed I couldn't!

It wouldn't be right,' Lizzie protested. 'A young lady like you . . . You'd be found out and then . . . You don't mean it, do you?'

'I won't be found out because I'll change my name. I'll be—let me see, Annie Fisher, I think. Yes, that sounds a nice reliable name, don't you think? You can tell me what sort of clothes I shall need and what my duties will be and how I ought to behave.'

'Miss Lynton, I just couldn't!' Lizzie gazed imploringly at Vicky. 'I daren't, it'd be wrong! I'd have to be untruthful! Couldn't you find something else to do, visiting the poor, or—'

'No.' Vicky caught sight of a book resting on Lizzie's shopping bag, a cheap novel whose highly-coloured cover depicted a golden-haired girl and a tall, handsome young man about to clasp her in his arms, and inspiration came! 'I'll tell you if you'll keep it a secret. I'm writing a book and the heroine is a nursemaid in a splendid household and I *must* know something of the work she will do.' She saw she had caught Lizzie's attention and went on swiftly: 'I'm not going on being a nursemaid, of course. I want only to get enough information for my novel.'

'Writing a book? That's wonderful, Miss. Of course you wouldn't know about service in a big house and all that. All the same—'

'The hero is a duke and wonderfully handsome,' Vicky invented rapidly, 'and he falls in love with—with Violet.'

'I've always thought Violet a sweetly pretty name,' Lizzie murmured. 'Do Lady Lynton and Sir Andrew know you're writing a novel?'

Vicky cast all scruples to the wind. 'Of course they do and they want me to be successful with it. But I must know what a nursemaid's life is like, you understand that, don't you?'

'Y-yes,' Lizzie sounded doubtful, 'but I can't say as I like deceiving folk.'

The girl's gloves were mended and cheap. Her hat had seen better days and the material of her coat and skirt was not of the best quality.

'Of course, I would not ask you to help me in this way without paying you something for your trouble, Lizzie. I'll give you thirty pounds if you'll do what I want.'

'Thirty . . .' Lizzie's eyes widened in dreams of a new hat . . . boots . . . a shirt for Jim . . .

'You'll need curtains and things for your new home,' the temptress murmured, 'or give the money to Jim for his business.'

'Well—if it's as you say, Miss . . . and your mama knowing and approving . . . and you not meaning to do it for long . . . and it's just for a book . . .'

'You chocolate is cold, I'll order another. Now listen carefully, Lizzie.'

Vicky arrived back at Grosvenor Place in a pleasantly serene frame of mind. Lizzie had written the letter without further fuss and it had been posted. She had also provided Vicky with some valuable information on the part she was to play and promised to help in other ways, swayed, possibly, by the promise of two dresses and a hat with ostrich feathers which Vicky had thrown in as further inducement.

'Now for Mama,' Vicky thought as she ran up the stairs to her mother's boudoir. 'How lucky it is I have such an inventive mind!'

Lady Lynton, deep in preparations for her trip abroad, agreed absent-mindedly not to expect letters from Norfolk when Vicky explained there would be nothing to write about.

'And Mama, *please* don't write to me. I've discovered

Aunt Matilda opens all the letters that come to the house and I simply couldn't bear it!'

'How very improper of her. However she was always somewhat eccentric. I wonder if I should buy a tropical umbrella; but green is *not* becoming to one's complexion. Oh dear, how complicated it all is.'

The days sped by, but not fast enough for Vicky. There was always the uneasy thought that she might be found out and everything ruined. She would not feel safe until her parents were on the steamer. Lizzie could be trusted, but there was the chance Lady Lynton might think it her duty to write to her aunt to thank her for having Vicky to stay with her.

Lady Lynton did write, but luckily she told Vicky who kindly offered to post it for her.

'I'm turning into a criminal, I'm afraid,' she thought ruefully as she disposed of the letter in a passing street-cleaner's cart. 'I don't even feel guilty any more. I am a liar, a deceiver and a most unsatisfactory daughter and I do not deserve to have managed things so well. But oh, I *am* glad I've managed them! And I'll take whatever punishment I have to afterwards.'

She was frank with herself except for one thing. She had shut her mind to the thought that it was the connection between the Falconers of Wellbury Court and the fascinating man she had seen at the ball that had put the whole idea into her head. She declined to think of him, and assured herself she would have taken Lizzie's place anywhere in England.

When she returned to the house she found her mother standing in a welter of dresses, jackets and frilled underwear, giving orders to her maid and advice to Harriet and Maud.

'*Not* the Paquin, Smith, I have worn it too often.'

'But the people in America have not seen it,' Harriet reminded her.

'That is true. Well pack it, Smith, and use plenty of tissue paper. Harriet, you must be prepared to attend divine service twice or perhaps three times on Sundays, I'm told the best families in Boston are extremely devotional. Smith, you will crush the feathers in that hat, be more careful. No Maud, I do not consider you need anything more in the way of dresses, it is nearing the end of the season and what you have will be sufficient.'

'But Flora entertains a lot, and we are to go to Henley.'

'Henley is not really for people like us,' her mother said, picking up a lace scarf. 'I never attend it.'

'Lord Burnley has arranged a party for it.'

Lady Lynton looked up. 'Has he? In that case you had better order something light and pretty from Madame Leblanche, she will know what is suitable. Smith, you must see to it that the clothes I shall need for Boston— we shall spend a few days there on the way back—are in the larger dress trunk, and the country clothes in the two smaller trunks.'

'Ten-gallon hat, flannel blouse and leather skirt,' Vicky suggested, 'and don't forget the snake boots, Mama.'

'Now Vicky, I am far too busy to listen to your nonsense. I have *so* much to do.'

'I just came to say I shall be staying here for a few days after you and Father leave. I have to do some shopping, and Aunt Matilda can't have me immediately.'

'Very well, tell the housekeeper, she will shut up the house after you have left. Did you get the double satin ribbon, Smith? Then start running it through those camisoles.'

Vicky slipped away. Things were going almost too smoothly. She hoped there would be no hitch in her plans before her parents left, and that Lizzie's conscience would not trouble her.

But Lizzie's conscience gave no further trouble. She supplied most useful information about what would be expected of an under-nurse, and also a list of clothes needed. Lady Falconer had answered the letter Vicky had dictated. She deplored the lateness of Lizzie's decision not to take the post offered, but accepted her 'cousin' as substitute since there was no time to engage anyone else. She sounded irritated, but also somewhat relieved at not having to look further, and Annie Fisher was instructed to arrive at Wellbury Station on Saturday, where she would be met by a groom.

The household was too busy to notice the parcels arriving for the youngest Miss Lynton. Vicky hid the print dresses, big white aprons, stout boots and brown holland coat. When she tried on the severely plain straw hat and gazed at herself in the looking-glass, she chuckled.

'If I met my dearest friend I wouldn't be recognised! But I must arrange my hair differently.' She pulled back the dark curly hair that seemed alive with vitality and not inclined to be smoothed into an Annie Fisher style. A hairnet might help, Vicky decided, and lots of hairpins.

She glanced at the garments spread on her bed and felt a twinge of dismay. Coarse cotton nightdresses with high collars and long sleeves, grey-boned stays, depressingly puritan cotton drawers and thick black cotton stockings.

'They will help me to *feel* I'm Annie Fisher,' she told herself firmly as she put away her trousseau for her entry into working life.

Sir Andrew and his wife and daughter set off in a fine flurry of last-minute instructions, suddenly-remembered parcels and gloomy prophecies of storms in the Atlantic by Lady Lynton. Maud was already with her sister Flora, and Harriet, looking calm and charming in her new travelling coat and sailor hat, hurried her mother into the waiting brougham before she could remember anything else she had forgotten or have further qualms about the trip.

Sir Andrew had called Vicky into the library the night before.

'Have you enough money, Vicky?'

She thought of the thirty pounds she had given Lizzie. 'I would like some more, please, Father.'

He pulled out his case. 'Lord knows what you women do with it all. You won't be able to spend much in Norfolk. I've arranged for you to be able to draw on my account up to a certain point, in case of an emergency.' He looked at her searchingly. 'I wonder if I oughtn't to take you with us; you're different from the other girls, *they* obeyed orders and behaved themselves. I sometimes think you're a changeling.'

'It's much too late to think of that,' she said hastily. 'And you know that even if I don't do all the things Mama thinks I should, I would never do anything really *wrong*.'

'Not wrong by *your* standards,' he said shrewdly. 'Well, Matilda will keep a tight rein on you and let us know how you are behaving.'

'Oh, she *never* writes letters,' Vicky explained, 'she told me so. I will tell you everything when you come home.'

And what, she wondered as she tucked the notes he had given her into her pocket, would follow if she revealed her duplicity? Horror? Punishment? Curtailment of liberty? But that was in the future and why bother about the future when the present was so exciting!

The house seemed dull and tomblike when she returned from seeing her family off at the station, and she had a sudden resurgence of doubt of what she was planning to do. *Was* she being very wicked deceiving her parents and behaving in a way she knew they would not approve? Would she hate working at Wellbury Court and perhaps being bullied by a grim head nurse and despised by the other servants? What if the children disliked her? What if she proved useless and was dismissed?

'I can always go to Aunt Matilda,' she thought. She had discovered from her Father that Aunt Matilda had in her youth run away with her brother's tutor and been rescued in time from a Gretna Green marriage, which was surely more serious than pretending to be a nursemaid.

'I'm not doing anything in the least like that,' Vicky thought, and was startled to find herself remembering a tall, dark-eyed man with a deep, lazy voice. She had not forgotten him, the man called Alex, although she had meant to. Those few moments at the door of Devonshire House stayed in her mind, ready to emerge with surprising intensity. She was too honest with herself to hide the truth.

'He *did* interest me. But I don't suppose I'll meet or even see him. Lizzie says the nursery staff and the children seldom see the rest of the household. I expect if I did see him I'd be horribly disappointed; and he may be engaged . . . no, he said he meant to remain free. Anyway, I'll probably be working too hard to think of anyone. Lizzie said she didn't care for the look of the head nurse at Wellbury Court.'

The housekeeper, occupied with putting away valuables and shrouding furniture in dust covers, did not notice Vicky slipping out of a side door dressed in her Annie Fisher clothes. A cab deposited her at the station where she found Lizzie, resplendent in the feathered hat.

'I had to come, Miss, in case you'd had a change of heart,' the girl said breathlessly. 'I still don't like it.'

'But I do, Lizzie. Don't worry, I shall behave beautifully and the children will adore me and I shall win over that dragon of a nurse, see if I don't.'

'Well, I'm sure I wish you luck, Miss. Me and Jim are going to stay with his uncle in Southend where there's a nice little grocery business that might suit us.'

'I wish *you* luck, Lizzie, and I am very grateful to you. And you look nicer in that hat than I did!'

She got into a third-class carriage and leant out of the window to wave to Lizzie until she was out of sight. Then she sank back with a sigh of relief. Now there was no going back. She did not intend to dwell any longer on her questionable behaviour, or what her friends and family might think. She was free! She was about to sample a new life that had nothing in common with the social round in which she had been compelled to take part. A wave of excitement caught her and she sat up, her lips parted and her eyes sparkling.

A figure in the corridor passing her window made her turn her head and she wondered for a second where she had seen the man before. But she had other things to think of and she lay back, sinking herself into the obscure little person of Annie Fisher. Her clothes—the holland coat, plain hat and thick boots—were correct, she knew.

'I'll have to be careful how I speak,' she thought. 'If anyone gets suspicious I could say I was educated by a well-off aunt—or perhaps I'm illegitimate and my father is well-born and sent me to a respectable school . . .' She broke into laughter, picturing her mother's scandalised face!

She had no real fears about her charges. She liked children and got on well with her nephews and nieces. The nurse would probably be her worst problem, but she would eventually realise she had a treasure in her new nursemaid!

She had to change from the mainline train into a local

one that would take her to Wellbury. As she waited on a side platform, she noticed the man she had seen in the train. She looked more closely at him and suddenly it came to her! He was the man who had been talking to the mysterious Alex at Devonshire House.

For a second she was uneasy, remembering how the man had glanced at her. Then she knew he would never recognise her, even if he had noticed her at Devonshire House, in her new personality of Annie Fisher with unbecoming clothes and hair dragged back and secured with hairpins and hairnet. She doubted if anyone would recognise her, and amused herself imagining what her friends would think if they could see her now.

When the train surged in, puffing ostentatiously as if to assure passengers it was just as important if not superior to the mainline giants, the man got into a first-class carriage and for the first time it struck Vicky he might be going to Wellbury Court. Was his friend Alex already there? Excitement tingled through her. She would not be likely to meet him, of course, yet might he not take an interest in his hostess's children and seek them out in their nursery . . . ? Her dream ended abruptly as she caught sight of her hands lying in her lap, encased in cotton gloves of quite remarkable hideousness! He would never notice Anie Fisher. To him she would be a meek, self-effacing figure in ugly clothes and quite without interest. This was a snag, and she must see what could be done about it, because she knew she meant to bring herself to his notice *somehow*!

Wellbury Station was small and had wallflowers and pansies growing in a bed edged with whitened stones. A stately Daimler waited outside the station entrance and Vicky watched the man she had recognised enter the car

and be driven off—almost certainly to Wellbury Court.
An elderly porter took her case out to a brake where the
groom, after she had got in, jerked the reins to set the
two horses off at a smart trot along a country road with
honeysuckle threading the hedgerows. Fields stretched
on either side and there were woods and farms to break
the monotony of the landscape. Vicky breathed in the
warm, sweet air, looking around her happily.

'You'll be the new nursemaid, I'm thinking,' the
groom, a short, grey-haired man, remarked.

'Yes, I am.' She wondered if she ought to call him 'sir'
and decided not.

'And what may your name be, Missie?'

'Annie Fisher.' Encouraged by his friendly manner
and something reassuring in his weathered face, she
asked: 'Is Wellbury Court very large?'

'Aye, large enough. The house is old-like, Georgian,
I'm told. The park's a fine one and we've a deer herd.'

'Are there guests staying in the house?'

'Oh aye, there's most always parties staying. Her
ladyship likes society and all that. Folks come from
London for the shooting.'

'But it is early for that.'

He turned to stare at her. 'Now how would a maid like
you know that?'

It was a slip, but she had an answer. 'I was brought up
in Scotland and I remember when the London gentlemen came for the shooting.'

The entrance to Wellbury Court was impressive. Two
stone gatehouses guarded the tall wrought-iron gates
that led into a long tree-lined avenue. On both sides
Vicky saw rolling grasslands stretching away to distant
woods. A herd of deer grouped under a wide oak turned
startled heads before racing away. When at last the
house came in sight she exclaimed in pleasure. Built
in Palladian style, the long frontage had dignity with-

out excessive grandeur and a simplicity of design that
satisfied the eye of the beholder.

The groom turned the horses into a side avenue that
led to the back of the house and kitchen quarters. The
wide cobbled yard had stabling on three sides and a
couple of stable boys cleaning harness turned to stare at
Vicky as she descended from the brake.

The groom took her case and she followed him into a
dark stone-floored passage and up a short flight of stairs.
A maid came out of a door carrying some clean linen and
the man said,

'Here's Mrs Brodmin's new lass. Take her to the
nursery. One of the boys can bring her case.' He looked
at Vicky, standing very straight and tall to disguise the
sudden panic that had seized her. 'You'll be all right,
Missie.' He lowered his voice. 'Don't you mind old
Brodmin's ways, she's crusty as a new loaf. Don't you
mind her.'

'I—I'll try not to.' With a feeling she was losing her
only friend in this strange new world she was entering,
she asked quickly: 'What is your name, please?'

'Obediah Dumble, and don't you forget it if you need
a bit of advice or help, my dear.'

'Oh, I won't,' she assured him, and gripping her
umbrella and stout leather handbag, she hastened after
the maid who was waiting for her impatiently at the bend
of the passage.

She soon became bewildered by the twists and turns of
passages and stairs and wondered how she would manage to find her way anywhere in this back-stair maze. At
last they came out onto a landing and the maid pointed
to a door and said, 'You'll find Nurse Brodmin in there,'
and left her.

Vicky paused to straighten her hat, then knocked
gently. She was bidden to enter and found herself in a
large bright room with wallpaper depicting nursery-

rhyme characters, a doll's house, rocking horse and a heavily-built woman sitting in a basket chair knitting. She looked up and subjected Vicky to a chilly stare through steel-rimmed spectacles before saying in a harsh and unpleasant voice,

'Annie Fisher, is it? Well, don't stand there gawping. You're late.'

'I'm afraid the train was not on time.'

'Keep your excuses to yourself, if you please.' She rose heavily, dropping her knitting. Vicky hastened to retrieve it and was not thanked. Mrs Brodmin inspected her coldly, her expression of disapproval deepening as she did so.

'So you're cousin to the chit who couldn't bother herself to come. Untrained, I suppose?'

'I'm afraid so, Mrs Brodmin, but I am very anxious to learn.'

'Oh, you'll learn all right, my girl, I'll see to that. You're here to work and don't you forget it.'

'No, I won't, Mrs Brodmin,' Vicky promised meekly, wondering if this was the usual reception of a newcomer to the nursery; or if Nurse Brodmin saw some reason to put her in her place.

The woman's next words confirmed this.

'I'll have no airs and high manners in this nursery, miss. Where'd you pick up that mincey way of speaking I'd like to know?'

By now Vicky had taken the woman's measure and knew continued meekness would merely goad her to further rudeness. She met the nurse's pale eyes, so unpleasantly enlarged by the thick spectacles, with composure as she said,

'My mother was a lady's maid in a large household; she trained me to speak properly.'

'Aping your betters! Well, I'm having nothing of that here, and mind you remember it. Your room's next door. You can unpack and then get the children ready for tea.'

The bedroom was small but bright and at least, Vicky thought with relief, she had it to herself. Her case was there and she unpacked swiftly and put on cap and apron and returned to the nursery where she found three children, two boys—obviously twins—of about nine, and a small girl she judged to be six or seven. They stared at her in silence for some minutes, then one of the boys asked,

'Are you Annie?'

'She is, and she's going to see you wash your hands properly, Master Giles, and Master Mark's too,' Nurse Brodmin told him.

'Mine are quite clean,' the girl said, her big brown eyes still fixed on Vicky.

'That's a good girl. Take the boys to the bathroom, Annie, and see they scrub those nails,' she turned to the twins: 'And if she don't do it right, you're to tell me, remember.'

They filed out of the door. Outside, Vicky said, smiling at the two solemn faces,

'You will have to show me where the bathroom is, I'm afraid. I've only just come here.'

'It's in here.' They led the way. Vicky stood watching them soap and rinse their hands.

Giles looked up in evident surprise. 'Aren't you going to scrub our nails for us?'

'Certainly not,' she said firmly, 'you are two big boys and I know you can do it yourselves.'

'We *like* to do it ourselves,' Mark remarked, grabbing the nailbrush, 'Only old Broddie always ends by doing it for us.'

'And she *scratches*,' Giles said, snatching the nailbrush away from his twin, 'once my fingers bled!'

'I got that brush first!' Mark protested. 'Give it back!'

'I won't!'

Vicky whisked the brush from Giles's hand. 'Which of you two is the elder?'

They stared, then Giles said: 'I'm ten minutes older than Mark.'

'Then you can use the brush first.' She gave it to him.

Slightly to her surprise they accepted her decision without argument. When they had finished, Giles looked up at her.

'You're *supposed* to look at our nails and do them again, but we won't tell on you.'

'Of course, we don't really *know* you yet,' Mark said gravely, 'but I think we may like you.'

'I'm pleased to know it,' Vicky said cheerfully. 'I like you.'

'I don't think Broddie likes us much,' Giles said thoughtfully. 'She says we're naughty.'

'I expect you are, sometimes.'

'Will you be cross when we're naughty?'

'Oh, I expect so, but not for long. Now let's go back to the nursery for tea.'

The first thing Vicky saw on entering the nursery was a slim, pretty and fashionably dressed young woman sitting in the window seat with the little girl in her lap.

'It's Annie Fisher, my lady,' the nurse said, 'as has come in place of the other girl.'

'I hope you will work hard and give satisfaction to Mrs Brodmin, Annie,' Lady Falconer said carelessly. She rose, setting the child on her feet. 'Lucy is looking pale, Nurse, I think she needs a tonic.'

'I'll see to it, my lady. She don't drink her milk like she ought, it's a fine struggle to get her to take as much as a sip.'

'Well you must go on trying, Nurse.' Lady Falconer rustled to the door as Mark asked,

'Can we come downstairs before supper, Mama?'

'No, Mark. Mama has guests, and some more will be arriving soon.'

'Can't we see them?'

'Now, don't be tiresome, Mark. Grown-ups don't want to be bothered with children—yes?' she looked up as a footman appeared in the doorway, 'What is it, James?'

'Please, m'lady, Lady Grange and Miss Grange, Sir Apton Fawley and Mr Alex Beaumont have arrived.'

'Gracious, already? Goodbye, children, be good and do what Nurse tells you.' Lady Falconer hurried out of the room, leaving the scent of carnations lingering in the air.

'Mr Beaumont has been here before,' Giles remarked, seating himself at the table where tea had been spread. 'He likes riding Papa's horses.'

'He's a nice man,' Lucy spoke for the first time, looking at Vicky. 'Once he gave me a ride on his horse.'

'Oh then he *must* be nice,' Vicky was relieved to find her voice steady, which was more than could be said of her heart! So he had arrived! His name was Alex Beaumont and he was in the same house as she was! But some of her excitement faded as she remembered the distance, wider and more impassable than an ocean, between them. She would never be in the drawing-room or he in the nursery unless luck took a hand in things. So far, the gods had favoured her; would they stretch their favour a little further and arrange a meeting between her and the man she had never forgotten?

'Nothing is impossible in this world,' she told herself as she began to butter a slice of bread for Lucy.

CHAPTER
THREE

IN the days following her arrival at Wellbury Court, Vicky had little time for further romantic speculation about Alex Beaumont. Nurse Brodmin found plenty for her to do and frequently scolded her for the inevitable mistakes she made. Vicky suspected many of the older nurse's duties were now assigned to her. Nurse Brodmin was lazy and given to taking long 'rests' in her room with her door locked in case she should be disturbed. Her manner did not soften towards her new nursemaid, nor would she admit that Vicky was quick at learning her duties and energetic in performing them, and the fact that the children were strongly in favour of Vicky was another source of irritation to her.

Work began at six o'clock when Vicky was expected to make tea and bring it to Nurse Brodmin, pull back the curtains and open windows in the nursery suite—Nurse Brodmin had a horror of 'night vapours', even in August—tidy and dust the nursery and schoolroom attached to it, set the table for breakfast, rouse the children and superintend washing and dressing.

Breakfast was brought up by the maid, Sue, a tight-lipped, severe young person who unbent under Vicky's friendly manner and warned her darkly of what she might expect from Nurse Brodmin.

'Sour as a cat she can be,' Sue confided as she put a loaded tray on the table. 'You watch out, Annie, 'specially when she has one of her turns, she's right nasty then.

'What sort of turns?' Vicky asked with some apprehension.

'Migrams, she calls 'em, but if you ask me, they're nothing but spiteful temper. She don't let on to her ladyship, of course; sweet as bee's honey she is to *her*.'

'I suppose she isn't very popular with the staff.'

'Popular?' Sue gave a short, sarcastic laugh, 'popular as poison, I'd say!'

Apart from welcoming Sue as a friendly soul, Vicky saw the chance of discovering something about the house-party. Sue's duties did not bring her into contact with the visitors, but gossip filtered down through the ranks of the staff and even so menial a person as Sue had quite a remarkable knowledge of what went on above stairs. In time, Vicky guessed, Sue would unbend further and there would be chances of an occasional chat when Nurse Brodmin was not about.

The boys had lessons in the morning with a retired schoolmaster, a bleakly conscientious man who was the butt of many mischievous tricks. The boys deeply resented having to work in what they considered to be holiday time and the fact that Nurse Brodmin had suggested the lessons to Lady Falconer as a means of keeping them out of trouble was another cause of their dislike of her.

Lucy was a quiet, somewhat stolid child whose response to Nurse Brodmin's scolding at mealtimes was to refuse to eat. When the nurse, having finished her extremely hearty meal, left the table to 'rest her digestion' in her room, Vicky found she could get Lucy to finish her meal by telling her fairy stories and Lucy's eyes grew round in wonder as she automatically ate up the rice and prunes she had rejected.

It was Vicky's duty to take the children for a walk in the afternoon on most days, as Nurse Brodmin was not fond of exercise. She was strictly enjoined to keep to that part of the park where it was unlikely they would meet any of the house-party. Evidently Lady Falconer believed in the children being neither seen nor heard, and the nearest Vicky came to seeing anyone was an occasional glimpse of a carriage or motor car bowling down the avenue, or horsemen cantering across the far side of the lake.

By the time her day was ended, a day of looking after the children, washing, ironing, mending, tidying and dusting and running errands for Nurse Brodmin, Vicky tumbled into bed with no thought but to rest her weary body and forget another such day lay ahead of her. Yet each morning she rose with fresh optimism and interest in the world she had chosen to enter, and felt no regrets at deserting her old, comfortable life.

In spite of Nurse Brodmin and the work, Vicky found much to enjoy. The children liked and confided in her. Sue brought scraps of information from below stairs that opened up a world as unknown to Vicky as an African jungle, a world geared to smooth efficient service that was accepted without question or notice by those it served; as *she* had once accepted it. In some ways it was a reflection of her own world, with its jealousies and snobbery. Distinction of class was rigidly observed from housekeeper down to the lowly boot-boy and tweenie, and woe betide the aspiring soul who overstepped the well-marked boundaries.

Vicky returned from a drive in the dog-cart with Lucy, having been sent to the village to buy some things for Nurse Brodmin. The drive had been delightful, with golden sun lighting stubbled fields and cottage gardens and a clear blue sky flecked with tiny clouds. A quick wind had whipped colour into her cheeks and set her spirits soaring and she arrived at the nursery door flushed and breathless after a race with Lucy up the stairs. As she opened the door, she saw the figure of a man kneeling on the floor with the two boys, surrounded by a network of toy railway lines. He was winding up a little engine and her heart gave a leap! Then the man turned and she saw he was not Alex Beaumont but the man she had noticed on the railway platform, the man Alex had called Thomas.

He smiled at her pleasantly. 'I'm afraid we have rather spread ourselves over your floor. Will the Great Western Railway be in your way?'

''Course it won't,' Giles exclaimed. 'Come on, Mr Craig, set the engine going or she'll be late at the junction. Annie won't mind, she's nice.'

'Broddie won't like it,' Lucy remarked. 'Did you bring that engine and all those railway lines, Mr Craig?'

'Yes, he did,' her brother told her, setting the engine on the rails and watching its progress as it rattled across the floor to the 'junction', 'and he has a present for you.'

The man rose. 'It's a doll's tea-set,' he told Lucy. 'I hope you will give a tea-party and invite me.' He took a large parcel off the table and gave it to Lucy who squealed with joy as she tore off the wrappings.

It was a charming little set of rose-patterned china and Lucy was busy setting out the tiny cups and saucers when the door opened and Nurse Brodmin stood staring at them with ill-concealed disapproval. The boys paid no attention, but Lucy looked up and clutched the tea-pot to her chest protectively.

'Mr Craig, I thought you said you wanted to take the boys out for a walk,' Nurse Brodmin exclaimed.

'We did walk, Nurse, but we got tired of it and I had a present for the boys which we wanted to set working,' he said easily.

'Well, it's time for their tea now, Mr Craig. Annie, you help the boys clear away the mess—and Miss Lucy, you can put away that tea-set, it's too good to be broken.'

'Oh, I won't break it, I *promise*!' Lucy looked imploringly at the nurse.

'We shall clear it all away presently, it is not yet four o'clock,' Thomas Craig said quietly. He did not look at Nurse Brodmin, but something made her hesitate before marching across the room, stepping over the railway lines, angry but defeated.

As she removed Lucy's coat and beribboned hat, Vicky cast an anxious glance at the man now busy showing the boys how to manipulate the points and gave an inward sigh of relief. He had not recognised her. Indeed, how could he possibly associate a nursemaid in a shapeless holland coat and unbecoming hat with the slim girl in lilac taffeta and velvet cloak among the guests leaving Devonshire House? The notion made her smile and she looked up to see the man rise to his feet and turn to ask,

'Are nursery rules desperately strict? Am I allowed to share the nursery tea, do you think?'

'I—I think you had better ask Nurse Brodmin,' she said, somewhat taken aback.

'Oh, please do stay and have tea with us!' Lucy begged. 'Don't let's ask her—' she looked around as the door opened and her mother entered. 'Mama. Mr Craig says he wants to have tea with us. He *can*, can't he? *Please* say he can!'

'My dear Thomas, what can appeal to you in nursery tea?' Lady Falconer protested. 'Bread and butter and plain cake. Alex told me you had taken the boys for a walk instead of riding with him.'

'He's brought us a train set and Mark and I have been playing with it,' Giles told her. 'If we promise to tidy it up afterwards, can Mr Craig stay to tea with us?'

'Well, I suppose so, if he insists.' She turned to Nurse Brodmin. 'Mr Craig will have tea with the children today.' Lady Falconer had evidently been visiting. Her

grey moiré dress suited her slim figure and her wide
straw hat was trimmed with roses and blue velvet ribbon.
'You really are a quaint creature, Thomas.'

'Because I sometimes prefer bread and butter and
plain cake to pâté sandwiches and cream éclairs?' he
asked, grinning at her cheerfully.

'Effie will miss your company,' she warned him lightly.

'Not while she has Alex to entertain her.'

'You are not to stay long, Thomas. Charles wants to
talk to you about this new tenants bill or something
dreadfully dull.' She turned to Nurse Brodmin who was
standing by the window, coldly disapproving. 'We are
going to Beechly Hall tomorrow and Lady Framton
wants me to bring the children, she has her grand-
children staying with her at present.'

'I don't like Gussie,' Mark said abruptly, 'and Emily
always teases Lucy.'

'She pulled my hair,' Lucy said. 'It *hurt*.'

'I bet it did,' Thomas Craig agreed. 'I give your
brothers my full permission to pull Emily's hair in
return.'

'Whoops! May we?' both boys cried and their mother
shook her head in reproof.

'Really, Thomas, I fear you will upset Nurse's disci-
pline.' Lady Falconer swept from the room and the boys
began to gather up the railway lines under Thomas
Craig's direction.

'What are you standing stupidly like that for, Annie?'
Nurse Brodmin's voice made Vicky start. 'Set the table.
Here's Sue with tea.'

Vicky hastened to obey before going to her room to
remove her coat and hat. She looked at herself in the
glass as she put on her starched cap, thinking Aunt
Matilda was right and indeed she was no beauty and any
good points she might have were obscured by the

hideous cap and ugly hair style. She did not observe the fine, delicate bones of her small face and the quaint pointed chin and mobile mouth, and was too accustomed to the wide, silvery-grey eyes and dark curling lashes to be aware of their unusual charm. Beauty, she was convinced, consisted of a softly rounded figure, golden hair and deeply blue eyes, rosebud mouth and porcelain complexion. Her creamy skin she thought colourless and her thick, rebellious curls a nuisance to control.

She was amused at how soon Nurse Brodmin's irritation faded and how she smirked when her unexpected guest remarked on the healthy appearance and good manners of her charges.

Vicky did not venture to join in the conversation, but she listened with interest to their guest's account of a party given for the tenants' children at the country seat of a well-known and aristocratic family.

'The Duke of Dalewater's seat, Fernleigh Towers?' Nurse Brodmin exclaimed, leaning forward until her heavy bust rested on the table. 'Isn't that where a valuable diamond tiara was stolen from one of the guests not long ago, sir? Were you there?'

'As it happened, I was.'

'Tell us about it,' the boys chorused. 'How did the burglars get in the house? Did the police catch them? Did they find any clues?'

'Giles and Mark say they want to be policemen when they grow up,' Lucy volunteered.

'A noble ambition. Yes, the police found some clues, but they didn't catch the thief.'

As he parried the boys' eager questions, Vicky studied him covertly. He was of medium height, broad of shoulder, with thick chestnut hair, a somewhat rugged face and blue eyes under rather heavy brows. A strong face and, she decided, a pleasant one. She would forgive him this time for not being Alex Beaumont.

After he had gone, the children played with the toys he had brought them. Then it was bath-time and bed. Lucy sat squirming under the torture of having her fair, straight hair rolled up in rags by Nurse Brodmin.

'You stay still, Miss Lucy. Don't you want to look pretty when you go to take tea with Lady Framton's little grandchildren?'

'No, I don't want to go.'

'We don't like Gussie and Emily,' Giles said, 'they never let us play with their toys.'

'Is Beechly Hall a fine place?' Vicky asked with interest. 'I should like to see it.'

'Well, you can put it out of your head,' the nurse snapped. 'You won't be wanted. *I* take the children tomorrow. You can get on with your work here.'

This was a disappointment. A visit to a neighbouring house would be a break in the monotony, but there was no chance of persuading the old nurse to allow her nursemaid to accompany her.

Vicky glanced at the nurse and saw she was fidgetting with Lucy's hair. Suddenly she said,

'You can do the last bit. My head's bad tonight, I'm away to bed—and I shan't want supper.'

'I'm sorry,' Vicky said. 'Is there anything I can do?'

'Just keep yourself out of my way, that's all!' The woman flounced out of the room and Vicky did not see her again that night.

Next morning, when she took in the nurse's tea, she wrinkled her nose distastefully at the stuffy atmosphere in the room. When she had put the tray down, she went to open the window.

'Leave it alone!' The command made her jump. The hump in the bed that was Nurse Brodmin heaved slightly. 'Don't dare draw the curtains. My head's still bad. It's my migraine. I'll have to stay in my room. See to the children and leave me alone.'

At breakfast, Mark asked hopefully: 'If Broddie is ill, does it mean we can't go to Beechly Hall?'

'I'm not sure—' Vicky broke off as Lady Falconer entered the room. She was in riding dress with her skirt looped over one arm. Vicky rose hastily.

'Where is Nurse Brodmin? She is to take the children early to Lady Framton's.'

When Vicky explained, Lady Falconer frowned impatiently. 'Oh, these stupid migraines! Really, at times I think . . . Well, you will have to go with the children, Annie. See the boys are clean and neat and Lucy wears one of her embroidered dresses and the muslin hat.'

'Very well, my lady.'

'And see you are tidy also.' Lady Falconer's eyes ran over the print dress and big apron. 'Do you have another dress?'

'No, my lady, at least, only one like this one.'

'Well, see it is clean.' She went out quickly and Vicky heard her call to someone: 'Tell Mr Beaumont I shall be ready to ride with him in half an hour.'

Since the nurse did not emerge from her room, Vicky supposed she was not interested in lunch. After the meal, there was the task of getting three disgruntled children clean and dressed in their best, a proceeding that took so much time that she had to change her dress swiftly and when she came to doing her hair, the pins slid and the hairnet tore. At last in exasperation she seized the comb and arranged her dark curls loosely and, clapping her hat on without bothering about hat-pins, hurried to gather children, wraps and clean handkerchiefs and shepherd her little flock down the back stairs to the stable yard where she was delighted to see her friend, Obediah Dumble, on the box of the smart little phaeton.

He touched his cap and smiled at her as she got in.

'I'm glad you are to drive us, Mr Dumble,' she said. 'Is it a long drive?'

'No more than 'bout five miles. Now, young sir, you leave them reins alone.'

'Can I drive for a bit of the way, Dumble?' Giles asked.

'We'll see about it. Likely your nurse won't allow you.'

'Oh, Annie will let us,' Giles assured him,' she lets us do lots of things old Broddie doesn't.'

'And we don't tell tales,' Mark added, ''cause she doesn't tell tales on *us*.'

The drive in the warm afternoon sunlight was very pleasant. Dumble let Giles and Mark take a turn at holding the reins which made up for some of their disgust at having to meet Gussie and Emily. Vicky's heart was quite delightfully light. How lucky that a migraine had given her this afternoon. She tried to feel sorry for Nurse Brodmin and failed rather badly and felt guilty, but not for long.

Beechly Hall was not as grand a mansion as Wellbury Court and the grounds were not so extensive. They were taken up to the nursery where the nurse, a big, fresh-faced country girl, greeted Vicky in a friendly manner.

''Tis too bad, Mrs Brodmin being laid low,' she said. 'I hear she's taken that way often, poor dear. You're new, aren't you? What's your name, please?'

'Annie Fisher. I've only been at Wellbury Court for—' Vicky swung around hearing Lucy squeal and saw a boy of about ten hastily drop one of the child's curls.

The nurse said sharply: 'Master Gussie, that's no way to treat your guests! You do that again and I'll have to tell your grandma.'

'She won't pay any attention to you, so *there*!' Gussie hunched his narrow shoulders and contorted his pasty face into a frightful grimace that made Lucy shrink back.

'I'm *so* glad you did that,' Vicky said, 'it's *much* prettier than your ordinary face!'

Gussie's furious stare made his nurse clap her hand over her mouth while Giles and Mark laughed delightedly. A small girl in a fussy pink muslin dress came into the room and stood staring at them.

'We're to take the children to the croquet ground,' the nurse said. 'Lady Framton has ordered a set of small mallets for them. We'll have tea in the summer-house as a treat.'

The croquet lawn lay to one side of the house, separated from the path by a low hedge. Soon the children were whacking balls energetically, if not often accurately, at the hoops. Vicky, watching them—she still did not trust Gussie—heard carriages arrive and the sound of motor tyres on the gravelled sweep before the house. So the Wellbury Court party had come.

A yell from the boys made her hurry to where Giles and Mark were clinging to their mallets which Gussie was attempting to wrest from them.

'You cheated!'

'No I didn't!'

'Yes you did—you're a dirty little cheat!'

'*You* cheated, I saw you kick the ball through the hoop!'

'I didn't . . . anyway, it's *my* croquet ground and I shan't let you play on it any longer!'

'Stop it this instant!' Vicky grabbed Gussie who promptly kicked her painfully on the shin. 'Give me those mallets!'

Before she could stop him, Gussie hurled himself at Giles and Mark and there ensued a wild mêlée of flying arms and legs and yells of rage. Vicky caught at the nearest arm and heard someone behind her say in an amused voice,

'Can I help? It looks a bit too much for you.'

She released the arm abruptly and stepped back, her eyes wide and colour flooding her face as she watched Mr Alex Beaumont proceed to disentangle the combatants with surprising swiftness and ease. He turned to smile at her.

'A lot of little savages, aren't they? I saw one kick you, is it painful?'

'N-not very,' she managed to stammer. He was even more devastatingly handsome and engaging than she remembered and he was having an even worse effect upon her heart! 'I'm very grateful to you.'

He released Gussie who fled, sobbing with rage, across the lawn and out of sight.

'I think you had better keep them separated for a time, Nurse,' he said.

Nurse! For a moment she had forgotten. Her heart sank as she thought of the picture she must make in her ugly nursemaid's coat and hat . . . Where *was* her wretched hat? She looked around, her hands flying to her disordered hair.

'A casualty of war,' he remarked, presenting the hat to her. 'I trust it has not suffered too severely.' He was not looking at the hat; his eyes were on her flushed face and tumbled curls and the long dark lashes that hid the silver-grey eyes as her gaze dropped before his.

'Thank you—sir.' She took the hat and turned quickly to the boys. 'You should not have fought like that, Giles and Mark.'

'He fought *us*,' Mark said indignantly, rubbing a bruised cheek. 'He said we cheated and we didn't.'

Alex Beaumont picked up Gussie's mallet. 'No you didn't, I was watching you. Come on, let's have a game before tea.'

Vicky retreated, her mind in a whirl. To have met him when she was dishevelled and struggling with three infuriated boys . . . *Could* anything have been worse?

'Well, yes, it could,' she thought, 'I might not have met him at all.'

The gods were on her side, even if they had not arranged things quite as she would have wished. She had come to Wellbury Court hoping to meet him and there was no use in pretending she had not. From the moment Lizzie had mentioned the name Falconer, and Devon, the strange, unsettling excitement had caught and held her.

Well she *had* met him, and remembering the sudden quickening of interest in his eyes, she knew they would meet again!

CHAPTER
FOUR

THE rest of the afternoon passed in a haze of conflicting emotions for Vicky. The thrill of meeting and speaking to the man who haunted her dreams, uneasiness at the feelings he aroused in her, and the dissatisfaction with herself for being so stirred by the meeting, made her wish she could be alone. But when the croquet game was over there was tea in the summer-house and further trouble with the boys, still resentful, and Lucy spilling milk down her dress and having to be taken to the house to be dried out. Finally Vicky piled them all thankfully into the phaeton and set off for home.

Obediah Dumble's enquiry as to how they had enjoyed themselves brought furious condemnation of their afternoon's entertainment from the children and the groom grinned sympathetically at Vicky.

''Twasn't much of a success, then, Missie?'

'It was dreadful,' she told him. 'The boys fought.'

'And that beastly Gussie kicked poor Annie,' Lucy chimed in. 'I saw him.'

'Does it hurt you much, Annie?' Giles asked.

Vicky glanced down and saw the slight swelling on her ankle. 'Well yes, it does a bit, I'm afraid. I will have a fine bruise there.'

'Next time I meet Gussie,' Mark growled, 'I'll kick him on *both* ankles, *hard*!'

Vicky pretended not to hear—and heard Dumble chuckle.

Nurse Brodmin was sitting in the basket chair, her

knitting in her lap, when they returned. Vicky thought she looked unwell. Her face was unpleasantly mottled, her eyes were red and her mouth hung slackly as she looked up.

'You can put the children to bed, Annie. I'm not up to it.'

'I'm sorry. Is there anything I can get you?' Vicky asked, a little anxiously. The nurse really did look very unlike her usual self. 'Perhaps you should go back to bed.'

'Aye, maybe I will.' She got up slowly, gripping the arms of the chair. 'My head is no better.' She swayed slightly and Vicky took her arm and went with her into the bedroom which smelt strongly of the sickly joss-sticks the nurse liked to burn, saying they cleared her head.

The children were tired and fractious and Vicky was glad when they were at last in bed and she could sink onto the wide window-seat and look across the gardens and lawns now full of shadows as night crept over the land.

Her ankle still pained her and she was wondering what she should do about it when someone knocked. She went to the door and saw Thomas Craig. He had the little toy engine in his hand and gave it to her saying,

'I had to do a bit of adjustment on it, but it goes well now.'

'Thank you, the boys will be pleased, Mr Craig.' She waited for him to go, but he stood looking at her for a moment before remarking that his friend Alex Beaumont had told him there had been a fight among the boys that afternoon at Beechly Hall.

'Alex said young Gussie kicked you. Does your ankle still hurt you?'

Vicky sighed. 'Everyone asks me that. Yes, I'm afraid it does, and it's a little swollen.'

'Put alternate hot and cold bandages on it,' he ordered, 'and rest it, keep your leg up.'

'How can I possibly do that?' she asked irritably. 'I happen to have work to do.'

'Let the old nurse do it,' he said promptly.

'She isn't well.'

'Then I'll mention it to Lady Falconer.'

She gasped, her eyes widening in dismay. 'Oh dear, you mustn't do anything of the kind! I promise I'll bathe it and rest it as much as I can. It is only a bruise.'

'There's a doctor in the village.'

She looked at him in exasperation, then suddenly began to laugh.

'You behave as if a bruised ankle is important.'

'It could be of importance to someone.' He nodded to her and turned away and she shut the door, still smiling, but with a warm little feeling of gratitude that anyone should be concerned on her behalf. Suddenly she caught her breath as understanding came, bringing a wave of hot blood to her face. Alex Beaumont had sent Thomas, his friend, to ask how she was! He was the 'someone' who knew she had been hurt and wanted to find out how bad the hurt was. Probably he had not found it possible to slip away from the bridge table or billiard room and had used his friend. She remembered the quickened interest in his face as she stood before him, flushed and with her dark curls tumbled about her face, and a little shiver of excitement ran through her. He had noticed her, and perhaps realised she was no ordinary nurse-maid! What would his next move be?

It was a game, an enchanting *divertissement*, a break in a life she found lacking in adventure and excitement, she told herself. Alex attracted her. Perhaps she was just a little in love with him. She had broken out of her old life in rebellion against its conventional rules of behaviour. She would have to return to that life, of course, but this was a charming little episode which she meant to enjoy to the utmost. Perhaps she would have met Alex sometime if she had remained in London, but how much more exciting and romantic it was to have met him like this!

She was smiling when Sue came in with her supper.

'My, you're looking fine and happy,' the maid remarked, setting down the tray. 'Someone left you a fortune? You ought to see that Miss Effie Grange as *has* a fortune, proper dull she looks tonight, James says.' Sue had an 'understanding' with James, the good-looking young second footman. 'She's setting her cap at that handsome Mr Beaumont. He plays bridge with her and turns over the music when she sings and goes riding with her and all. But he's away tonight, and she's moping if you ask me, pore thing.' She sighed gustily. 'Disappointed in love, probably, 'spite of her wealth.'

Vicky agreed the path of true love was seldom smooth and ate her supper with good appetite. Earlier she had gone to ask Nurse Brodmin if she wished for anything and found the door locked and heard stentorian snores in answer to her enquiry.

The August moon was radiant in a purple sky, squandering its silver magic over the land. Vicky, looking from her bedroom window, felt a sudden urge to wander through the silent gardens, to smell the damp, cool earth and listen to the sleepy rustle of birds in the bushes and distant, haunting cry of an owl. But such behaviour was not at all proper for a young nursemaid, and she turned with a sigh to her bed, to dream of dark, amused eyes and hear again Thomas Craig saying: 'It could be of importance to someone . . .'

If Nurse Brodmin's appearance had improved next morning, her temper had not. She snapped at the children and scolded Vicky and spoke sharply to Sue for bringing breakfast five minutes late, causing that affronted young woman to sniff fiercely before flouncing out of the room and slamming the door behind her.

Vicky was relieved when Lady Falconer arrived to say the children were to be brought down to tea that afternoon.

'Miss Grange wishes to see the children,' Lady Falconer said. She thrust out warning hands as Lucy ran to her. 'No, Lucy dear, don't touch Mama's pretty gown, your hands will be sticky. Tea will be on the terrace, Nurse. Annie had better come with you, she seems to manage the boys well.'

'She stopped us fighting Gussie,' Giles said, somewhat resentfully.

'It was Mr Beaumont who stopped us,' his twin corrected him. 'He played croquet with us afterwards when Gussie ran away.'

'Well it was very naughty of you to fight,' his mother said vaguely. 'Do you feel better now, Nurse Brodmin?'

'Yes, thank you, my lady.'

Vicky was aware of pleasant excitement. She would be able to observe members of the house-party before they left on Monday morning. There was, Sue told her, to be a lull in entertaining until the next arrivals. If this afternoon was a success, perhaps Lady Falconer would allow the children to appear downstairs more often. It would be amusing, Vicky thought, to view society from her present lowly position.

For once, she arranged her hair softly around her face and placed the unbecoming cap as far back as possible. Nurse Brodmin's mouth tightened when she saw her, but there was no time for her to complain.

'I expect it will be horribly dull,' Mark remarked. 'Grown-ups ask you stupid questions about your lessons and what toys you like playing with.'

'That reminds me,' Vicky said,' you must thank Mr Craig for mending your engine.'

'I have. We met him when Dumble was giving us riding lessons and he asked us how your ankle was and we told him you were rushing about just like always.'

'Was Mr Beaumont with him?'

'No, he was riding with Miss Grange in the park.'

A ripple of conversation punctuated with light laughter greeted the nursery party as it came onto the long stone terrace. The children joined the group of visitors clustered around the tea table and were exclaimed over and admired. Vicky, staying modestly in the background, watched Lady Grange's heavily be-ringed hand smoothing Lucy's curls and longed to tell her ladyship how much Lucy was hating it. Lady Grange, encased in brown satin and ecru lace, was a short, plump woman with a sluggish expression. Her daughter was pretty, slender and graceful, with a fashionably languid manner and restless eyes. Vicky saw her turn her head sharply when Thomas Craig arrived on the terrace and caught the fleeting disappointment that crossed her face.

'Isn't Alex joining us?' Lady Grange asked her hostess.

'I believe so. He has been looking at the balcony on the west side and says work is required on it as some of the wood is rotten.'

'Tiresome fellow,' her husband remarked, helping himself to a wafer of bread and butter, 'I suppose it will have to be done one day.'

It was the first time Vicky had seen the owner of Wellbury Court. Sir Charles did not impress her; sleek, straw-coloured hair and a weak chin gave his face a vacuous look.

'Really this weather is *too* deevy,' a woman in pink muslin exclaimed. 'Ah, here comes our naughty Alex.'

He ran lightly up the steps of the terrace and bent to murmur an apology to his hostess before accepting a cup of tea and seating himself in the empty chair beside the no longer languid Miss Effie Grange.

It was a pity, and rather unwise, Vicky thought critically, for the heiress to show her preference quite so plainly and to colour and drop her eyes when Alex Beaumont bent to whisper something to her. Suddenly he raised his head and, as their eyes met, Vicky felt her heart skip a beat.

A few minutes later Lady Falconer signalled to Nurse Brodmin to remove the children. Miss Grange, who had demanded to see them, was no longer interested.

As she followed the nurse through the hall, Vicky heard a step behind her and turned quickly.

'How is your ankle?' Alex Beaumont asked.

'Oh, much better, thank you, sir.' Her cheeks were warm with the quick blood that flew to them. 'It was only a bruise.'

'A painful bruise, I think. The boys tell me you are Annie Fisher and you have not been here long.' He came nearer, keeping his eyes on her. 'I confess I am curious to know *why* you are a nursemaid, Miss Fisher.'

'*Annie!*' There was no mistaking Nurse Brodmin's anger.

'Because . . . I like being one,' Vicky murmured and hurried after the nurse and children.

So he *had* known she was not a servant. How much had he guessed? How much would she tell him when they next met—for they would certainly meet again. Would she hint at the truth or keep him guessing? She raced up the stairs with the boys, her heart singing.

Her happiness stayed with her in spite of the nurse's ill-temper and a burst of naughtiness by the boys, and a silent supper with a brooding Nurse Brodmin who rose abruptly saying she was tired and went to her room.

Vicky waited for the usual click of the lock and noticed it did not come.

She was dreaming of her father surrounded with the bones of the Tyrannosaurus Rex when something awoke her. She lay for some minutes, wondering what it was. It came again, an odd mumbling sound.

Now wide awake, she jumped out of bed and hurried to the children's rooms where she found all quiet. Then she noticed a light under the nurse's door and after a moment's hesitation, she turned the door handle gently and peered in.

Nurse Brodmin sat in a chair. She had not undressed and her cap was over one ear. Her heavy face was flushed and she was muttering hoarsely to herself as her unsteady hands fumbled with a glass. The room stank of whisky and two bottles, one empty, stood on the table beside her.

For a second shock held Vicky motionless. Then she ran forward and took the glass from the woman's hand.

'Nurse Brodmin, what are you doing?' But it was unfortunately quite obvious what she had been doing and what, Vicky now realised with a fresh shock, she had been doing for some time. A cupboard was open, revealing several more bottles and a packet of the scented joss-sticks which had been used to disguise the aroma of whisky in the room. 'You had better go to bed.'

'Head bad . . . mush—must take something for . . . m'head,' she hiccupped loudly and began to giggle.

It was a struggle to get the woman to undress and into her bed but Vicky, controlling her repugnance, managed it at last. She flung open the windows, put the bottles in the cupboard and shut the door and went to her room to think what she ought to do.

Obviously the woman was unfit to be in charge of children. If her drinking was getting worse there was real danger for all of them. Did the other servants know or suspect something, she wondered? They knew most of what went on in the house and might well recognise the nurse's 'migraines' for what they really were.

'Ought I to tell Lady Falconer?' She began to pace the room restlessly. 'I wouldn't like to be the cause of her being dismissed without a character. But she must not stay, she will be found out eventually. If I talked to her . . . but she wouldn't listen and she would probably get *me* dismissed for impertinence.'

Her sleep was broken for the rest of the night and there were dark shadows under her eyes next morning when she went to wake the children. She went in search of Sue and asked for a pot of strong coffee. When it came, she poured out a cup and took it into the nurse's room.

Nurse Brodmin was sitting up in bed and shocked pity mingled with disgust as Vicky saw the swollen face and red-rimmed eyes and slack mouth.

With an effort to sound normal, she said: 'We're having coffee for a change, Nurse Brodmin. I've brought you a cup, it will do your headache good.'

The nurse looked at her dully for a moment. 'Thank you.' She took the cup, but her hand shook and she spilt some of it.

'Let me hold it,' Vicky said quickly and guided the cup of hot black coffee to the nurse's mouth and watched her gulp it down and then lie back, her eyes fixed on Vicky's face.

'Don't go . . .' She put out a shaking hand. 'Oh dear God, I feel so bad! My head is splitting!' She sat up with an effort. 'Annie, what happened last night? I—I can't recall . . .'

'You woke me up and I found you sitting in the chair and—and I made you undress and get into your bed.' Vicky avoided looking at the ravaged face.

'Well, I won't pretend,' the nurse said heavily. 'Give

me some more of that coffee. I suppose you're shocked. Your prissy little mind don't know how a woman has to help herself the best she can when things get too much for her. No doubt but you'll be running to tell her ladyship and getting me sent off like I was a criminal!'

'I shall not tell Lady Falconer,' Vicky told her, 'but I am afraid you must leave Wellbury Court, Nurse Brodmin. You cannot stay here in charge of the children. You will be found out eventually and that will be much worse for you than if you make some excuse to leave. I am truly sorry to have to say this. I don't know how long you have . . .'

'I've been this way for more than I'll tell. I had trouble, bad trouble, when my brother died sudden and I had to take on his children till they were grown. There was little money—and I had other troubles. A man wanted to marry me, or so he said—but he went off. I took to alcohol for comfort, it helped me through a bad time,' she looked out of the window and something sad and hopeless in her face sent a wave of pity through Vicky. 'I meant to give it up when I come here, but I couldn't, it had a hold on me, you see. I've known it would end something like this.'

'Have you anyone, a relation perhaps, who could help you?'

'There's my sister, she's helped me before. She works in a hospital. I'll go to her, she's a decent kindly creature.' She pushed aside the bedclothes. 'Bring me another cup of that coffee while I dress. I'll speak to Lady Falconer this morning and say . . .' She looked at Vicky, suddenly pitiful in her shame, 'What will I say, Annie?'

'You must tell her you have not felt well for some time,' Vicky said gently, 'and you find the work here too much for you and wish to leave at once. I promise I will not say anything about last night. I'll bring you some coffee and toast, you must eat something, and I'll help you to dress.'

'You're a little lady, Annie. I've always known it and I didn't like you for it. Lord knows what you're doing as a nursemaid.'

The boys were with their tutor and Lucy was playing with her doll's house when Lady Falconer came into the nursery looking both irritated and upset.

'It is really *too* annoying! Nurse Brodmin insists on leaving at once! What on earth are we to do?'

'I am afraid she is not at all well, Lady Falconer,' Vicky said.

'She looks quite dreadful. But to leave at a moment's notice, and just when I find I have to take the children on a visit to my mother . . . Oh, it is really *too* impossible.' Lady Falconer sank into a chair and gazed despairingly at Vicky. 'My mother is not feeling well and, as usual, thinks she is dying and insists I take the children to Dorset for a few days. And now *this*!'

'Are we going to Grandmama's?' Lucy asked with interest. 'I like going there.'

'I simply do not see how we *can* go, now that Nurse Brodmin is leaving this afternoon,' her mother moaned.

'Annie can take care of us,' Lucy said. 'We like her *much* better than Broddie and the boys do what she tells them.'

Lady Falconer turned to stare at Vicky as if seeing her for the first time.

'I wonder . . . Could you manage to get the children ready in time, Annie? We must leave tomorrow morning.'

'Oh yes, Lady Falconer. I'll pack this afternoon.'

'In that case . . . I really believe you'll do instead of Nurse Brodmin, Annie. She has not been satisfactory for some time, you know. These migraines . . . I suppose I shall have to find another nursemaid when I return.'

Vicky had an inspiration. 'Would you consider Sue, the under-housemaid, Lady Falconer? She is a very good worker and the children like her.'

'Very well,' Lady Falconer looked relieved, 'we can try her. You are a strange girl, Annie. You do not look or speak like a nursemaid.'

Vicky hastened to bring out the lady's-maid mother and her early training in refinement which appeared to satisfy her ladyship.

Sue was highly delighted with her promotion and came to thank Vicky for suggesting it and Vicky took the opportunity to ask what members of the house-party had left that morning.

'They're all leaving except the two gentlemen, Mr Craig and Mr Alex Beaumont. Lady Grange and her daughter will be coming back for the big dinner-party and ball that's being planned. Proper grand it'll be, James says, with all the gentry from around at it. There'll be London guests coming for it too. We'll see some fine fashions, I'll warrant, and Lady Grange will be wearing her famous emerald necklace, James says. Laws! I've been gossiping too long! Housekeeper wants me.' She fled, leaving Vicky with the delightful knowledge that Alex Beaumont would be at Wellbury Court when she returned.

CHAPTER
FIVE

VICKY was busy for the rest of the day. Sue had to be coached in her duties, the children's clothes inspected, mended and packed for the visit to Mrs Dreyer, Lady Falconer's mother, who lived outside Dorchester at Riverside House. She was determined to show Lady Falconer how suitable she was for the position of head nurse.

The children talked of their grandmother at tea.

'She's very old and wears black and she cries,' Giles announced, spreading strawberry jam thickly on his slice of bread and butter.

'Cries?' Vicky echoed, somewhat startled. 'Why should she cry?'

'She cries when we come,' Mark told her, 'and she cries when we go away. Don't eat all the jam, Giles.'

'Broddie doesn't let you put all that jam on your bread,' Lucy remarked primly.

'She isn't here any more,' her brother told her. 'Annie lets us do lots of things old Broddie didn't. I'm glad she's gone away.'

'I shall not let you be naughty while you are at your grandmother's,' Vicky said firmly.

Excitement at the coming visit made the children restless and getting them to bed took time, even with Sue's help. When she had finished her supper, Vicky also felt restless and the longing to be out in the garden was too strong to be resisted. Leaving Sue with her novel, she slipped out into the cool silence of the night.

A wind carrying a hint of rain would keep the guests indoors and she felt free to wander through the rose gardens, sweet with scent from the sleeping blossoms, across the little Italian sunken garden with its pretty marble Cupid holding his spouting vase, and into the shelter of the long yew walk where the hedges rose in high walls on either side.

Her feet made no sound on the grassy path and she felt her restlessness slip from her as she walked, letting her thoughts drift where they would. A turn in the path gave her a view of the west side of the house and the balcony that ran along it, an architectural embellishment added by a former owner and not completely in keeping with the style of the house.

Someone had spoken of the balcony . . . Sir Charles had complained about Alex Beaumont's remarks on the balcony's condition. Several bedrooms opened onto it. If it was really unsafe, it could be dangerous, Vicky thought, regarding it critically.

She turned away and said 'Oh!' in a startled voice. In the faint light she saw the figure of a man standing watching her. The scent of his cigar reached her as he drew nearer and she knew who it was before he spoke.

'A beautiful night,' Alex Beaumont murmured, 'but dark. However, the clouds are moving fast and we shall soon see the moon. Are you enjoying your stroll in the garden, Nurse Annie Fisher?'

'Very much, thank you,' she said composedly. She could not see his face clearly, but from his voice she knew he was smiling. 'I have been busy all day in the nursery.'

'Ah yes, Lady Falconer is taking her children to visit her mother, I believe. Tomorrow, isn't it?'

'Tomorrow morning.' She watched the end of his cigar glow like a tiny ruby star.

'And you came out to be refreshed by the night air.

You know, the river looks extraordinarily beautiful by night; may I suggest we take a look at it?'

She hesitated, tasting the delight of knowing he wished her to go with him. Of course, if she were found out there could be trouble for her. But who would know? She knew *he* would say nothing. It was a tempting prospect, too tempting to be resisted!

'Very well,' she said, 'but I must not be away too long.'

They left the shadowy path between the yew hedges and strolled through a copse of silver birch and out into the park and saw the shimmer of water. The clouds were thinning and a faint silvery light made magic of the trees swaying gently before the breeze and the wide stretch of greensward around them.

He said abruptly: 'Who are you? Is your name really Annie Fisher? What made you come here as a nurse-maid? I'm sorry if I'm being too curious, but I can't help it. I keep wondering about you and, being an obstinate man, I want to know the truth.'

They had come to the river path. She stood watching the slow swirl of water around the tall reeds. She was without her cap and the breeze ruffled her curls gently. Abruptly she raised her strange and lovely eyes to his as a mocking little smile curved her lips.

'So you suspect a mystery? It would be a pity to dispel it.'

'But I want to know,' he said vehemently as he tossed his cigar into the water. 'I must know who you are—and why are you pretending to be a servant here.'

'Once a mystery is explained it becomes common-place. I think I shall let you continue to be curious, Mr Beaumont.'

'But why? If there is a secret, I'll not give you away, I promise. *Are* you Annie Fisher?'

'Of course I am. And it is time I returned to the

house.' She swung around and began to walk swiftly along the path to the birch grove. A mischievous spirit had seized her. So he was intrigued with Annie Fisher? Then she would let him wonder a little longer. Her eyes were dancing and her lips parted in a smile as he came up to her.

'Wait!' He caught her arm. 'Why won't you tell me? Is there some reason why you had to take menial work? Were you forced into it?'

The touch of his hand was sending shivers through her and she said, a little breathlessly,

'There was a—a reason. I wasn't forced, but I had to find some kind of work to do and as I am not very accomplished I chose to be a nursemaid. But I have been promoted,' she tilted her head to look up at him. 'I am to be head nurse now that Nurse Brodmin has left.'

'But you should not be a nurse at all,' he exclaimed. 'It is obvious you are—'

'An excellent nurse who must return immediately to her charges,' she said lightly, despite a jumping pulse. 'Please let me go.'

Before she could move away he had caught her by her shoulders. As she met his dark eyes she whispered: 'No! Let me go . . .'

Her words were smothered as she felt his mouth on hers in a swift, hard kiss. Then he released her, so abruptly that she stumbled and put her hand to the silvery bark of a tree to prevent herself falling as she heard him say sharply,

'Thomas! What in hell are you doing here?'

She instinctively shrank back into the shadows as Thomas Craig walked forward. Had he seen her? It was dark in the little wood and it was unlikely he had recognised her. He was not looking in her direction. She waited, her heart thudding against her ribs, as he strolled up to Alex and said coolly,

'I found it hot in the house so I decided to take a walk.'

His back was to her. Like a slim ghost, Vicky slid away between the trees. Once in the gardens she picked up her skirts and ran.

Sue was nodding over her romance. 'You look all flushed-like, Annie. What have you been doing out there?'

'I walked down to the river. I realised it was late so I—I ran back.' She put her hand to her disordered hair. 'I'm going to bed, and so must you, Sue. We have to be up early tomorrow morning, remember.'

She stood for some minutes in the dark in her room, listening to her heart's quick beat and trying to calm her racing blood. How dare he treat her like that! As if she had been a common maid . . . but he knew she was not! Had he been angered by her refusal to explain who she was and so taken his revenge? Or was it something deeper than that? Was the handsome, popular Alex Beaumont falling in love with her?

When she had lit the gas, one glance in the looking-glass made her turn away swiftly. Her flushed face and starry eyes told a story she was not yet ready to read.

She lay awake for a long time. If Thomas Craig had not appeared just at that moment . . .

'I'm glad he *did* come,' she told herself, 'or I might have told Alex everything.'

She knew she was *not* glad that Thomas Craig had chosen to appear at that particular moment, a moment she would not forget, and his presence had been unwelcome. What was he doing, prowling around in the woods at that time? Had he been spying on his friend? Did he suspect him of having an assignation with someone? What business was it of his, anyway? He was a prying, Peeping Tom!

Perhaps the two men were not such close friends after

all, she thought as she tossed restlessly in her bed. They were so different. Alex, handsome, magnetic and mocking, who could set her heart racing, and Thomas, stocky, calm and completely ordinary, whom she had liked but now liked no longer. She wondered what explanation Alex had given, or if he refused explanation and castigated his friend for his unwarranted interference. The latter was the most likely and she hoped Thomas Craig was feeling thoroughly ashamed of himself!

With the memory of Alex's kiss to haunt her, how could she sleep? But sleep she did eventually and woke to find Sue pulling the curtains aside to let in a thin grey light that did nothing to cheer her spirits.

As she dressed the children and gave them breakfast, thoughts and memories teased her mind. Would she see Alex before she left Wellbury Court? Would he find an excuse to follow her? The last thought brightened the dull morning for her somewhat.

Lady Falconer and the two boys were to travel in the limousine, and Vicky, Sue, Lucy and the luggage were to follow in the carriage.

When she brought the two boys to the front door to join their mother, Vicky was both surprised and annoyed to see Thomas Craig sitting beside the chauffeur. Surely he was not going with them to Dorset? It was Sue who gave her the explanation.

'James says Mr Craig is some kind of relative to old Mrs Dreyer and she's right fond of him.'

Exasperation filled Vicky. The wretched man seemed to appear whenever he was not wanted. She could very well do without his presence, even though it was not likely she would be seeing much of him.

She watched him warily as he spoke to the boys, wondering if indeed he had seen her with Alex Beaumont last night, but when he saw her he nodded and his expression did not change. She was relieved, but still she resented his presence. If only it could have been Alex . . . But, of course, she was not pleased with him either. He had behaved unforgivably, grabbing her and kissing her like that . . . She felt her face flame and turned away. Thomas Craig had most annoyingly observant eyes.

Riverside House stood on rising ground above the river and looked across woods and fields to the distant roofs and spires of Dorchester. The house was large and rambling with a comfortable air about it. The rooms assigned to the children were spacious and sunny and after she had unpacked, Vicky was told to take the children to the drawing-room to meet their grandmother.

Old Mrs Dreyer was ensconced in a large, high-backed armchair, a tiny plump figure wearing a lace cap and black silk dress heavily ornamented with braid. As the children advanced to meet her she produced a handkerchief and applied it to her eyes.

'The dear children! So sweet . . . The boys resemble their dear grandfather! I find it so affecting . . .' She sobbed quietly for some minutes, then blew her nose, tucked away the handkerchief and smiled at the children standing patiently before her. 'Now dears, come and kiss Grandma.'

As Vicky was about to withdraw, she was called back and asked if she found all she wanted in the rooms and what time the children required breakfast. When she replied, she found Mrs Dreyer's eyes fixed on her in lively curiosity.

'I believe you are head nurse now? You are very young, but my daughter tells me the old nurse left unexpectedly and you have proved yourself capable of caring for the dear children.'

'I am gratified with Lady Falconer's opinion,' Vicky murmured.

Mrs Dreyer turned her head. 'Ah, Thomas. You must help me to entertain the dear children . . .'

As Vicky slipped from the room she could not escape hearing Mrs Dreyer saying,

'You know, Thomas, that young woman is not at all the usual class of nurse. Her appearance and the way she spoke . . . Have you noticed her eyes? *Quite* beautiful.'

Vicky enjoyed the three-day visit more than she had expected. True, her thoughts still persisted in returning to Alex, and the memory of their last meeting brought a mixture of emotions, none of which she could clearly define. But she was too busy to give much time to what had happened and what possibly might happen in the future. Mrs Dreyer had arranged picnics and visits to neighbours for her grandchildren and Vicky had to attend all of them.

Sometimes Thomas came too, and, although she did not like him any longer, Vicky had to admit he was extremely popular with the children, although he never appeared to make any effort to please them. She was extremely glad of his company on one occasion when Giles tried to pick some bullrushes and managed to fall in the river. Thomas scooped him out with the minimum of fuss, and administered a scolding which the boy accepted with unusual meekness.

Mrs Dreyer wept when told of the incident, being greatly upset by the thought of what *might* have happened if dear Thomas had not been there, and she wept afresh when Giles told her he had wanted the bullrushes for her. Lady Falconer spent her time visiting friends in the town and was patently anxious to return to Wellbury Court.

'There's the ball to be thought of,' Sue declared. 'Ever so grand it will be, mark my words. Lady Grange and her daughter and a parcel of fashionable folk from London are coming for it.'

'I don't suppose we shall see anything of it,' Vicky sighed.

'Well, Lady Falconer may let the children stay up to watch the dancing from the terrace,' Sue said hopefully. 'There'll be ever such fine dresses and jewels. Make your mouth water, it will, Annie.'

Preparations for the ball were already in hand when they returned to Wellbury Court. Lady Falconer at once became unusually busy and was often closeted with the housekeeper and butler. Sue brought news of menus being planned, and hot-house flowers being brought to perfection, and an orchestra being engaged to come from London. James, the second footman, was a most useful source of information.

Lady Falconer, on one of her infrequent visits to the nursery, was besieged with pleas from the three children and finally agreed to allow them to stay up late and view the ball for a short time from the terrace on condition that they wrapped up well and behaved themselves before the great event.

Vicky had not met Alex Beaumont since her return from Mrs Dreyer's, but she had seen him riding in the park with Sir Charles and Lady Falconer. She became restless, and angry with herself for the feeling of impatience which she should *not* be feeling after the cavalier way he had treated her. Had she, she wondered in some dismay, *wanted* him to behave as he had? Surely not! He had been extremely impertinent. Of course, someone in her lowly position should *not* have walked to the river with him. He knew that and knew she had wanted to go with him. Was that why . . .

At this point her feelings became so mixed that she firmly turned her mind to other matters and agreed to Giles's demand that they went on a picnic to a farm where the boys could ride on the backs of the big shire horses as they brought in the harvest. Lady Falconer gave her permission and Obediah Dumble brought around the dog-cart after lunch.

'Things going nice and smooth, I hears,' he said as Vicky and the children climbed in. 'Doing Mrs Brodmin's work and doing it well you are, Missie. 'Twas as well the poor creature went,' he added reflectively, touching the pony with the whip, and Vicky wondered how much he, and the other servants, had known of the old nurse's weakness.

She saw the two horsemen before they saw her.

'It's Thomas! Hello, Thomas!' the boys shouted and waved their caps. 'We're going to the farm for a picnic!'

The horsemen cantered up to the trap and Vicky found herself looking into the dark eyes she remembered all too well. Alex looked even handsomer in riding clothes than in country tweeds. Thomas looked a solid country squire and she recalled with some surprise that someone had told her he was a London barrister of good standing.

'Come with us, Thomas,' the boys pleaded. 'We're going to ride the hay horses and feed the ducks and chickens and see a baby calf.'

'We're having a nice picnic,' Lucy offered the bribe brazenly, 'there are *chocolate biscuits*!'

'My favourite picnic food,' Thomas declared. He looked directly at Vicky. 'Am I permitted to attend the feast?'

'I—I suppose so,' she replied uncertainly, 'although I can't see why you should want to, Mr Craig.'

'Thomas's interests are deplorably earthy ones,' Alex drawled. 'He will discuss crops with farmers for hours if you let him, so I shall be obliged to come with him and see he does not disrupt the poor man's work.'

The little cavalcade started off, Thomas on one side of the dog-cart and Alex on the other, smiling down at

Vicky's faintly flushed face. She felt excited, yet uneasy. She did not trust the feeling he could arouse in her—it was too strong, too unsettling—and she had not forgotten their last meeting. Stealing a glance at him from under her long lashes, she wondered if he had forgotten. She could tell nothing from his face or manner.

The farmer's wife welcomed them and gave the children cups of fresh milk and pieces of warm gingerbread. Then Thomas took the boys off to the stables and Lucy went with the farmer's wife to feed the chickens and see the new calf.

'I don't suppose you are particularly interested in farm animals,' Alex said, turning to Vicky.

'Oh yes, I am,' she said perversely, 'I think I shall help to feed the chickens.' She made a move to go but was arrested by his hand on her arm.

'But I am *not*. I'm a great deal more interested in a certain naiad with sea-maiden's eyes and a most distressing habit of hiding herself from me.' His fingers tightened on her arm, his eyes suddenly intent, and the mockery she half feared to see was gone. 'I must talk to you. Come.'

Crushing down a suspicion that she was being unwise, she let him lead her across the rough grass to where a small stream rippled and surged around the broad stepping-stones. He helped her across, keeping hold of her arm, and they followed a track that led them through a spinney and out to a wide view of fields and woods and distant farms.

Vicky stood looking around her. 'We could have our picnic here, the children would be able to run around.'

'But not fall into the stream,' he said. 'I believe Thomas has already fished one of them out of a river.'

'Yes, at Mrs Dreyer's. I was grateful to him, he acted so quickly and efficiently.'

'Oh, Thomas is pretty efficient, I grant you, although I

doubt if he is very quick. A slow brain but steady. A sturdy, honest and reliable character, our Thomas.'

Something faintly patronising in his tone made her say,

'The children are very attached to him, he knows how to get along with them.'

'But of course he does. He is a trifle childish in himself. There is no sophistication in his nature. A simple soul in many ways.'

She looked at him. 'But a good friend?'

'Oh yes. I've known him for many years, we were at Eton and Cambridge together. But why are we talking about Thomas? I want to talk about *you*.' He hesitated, then went on quickly, 'I wish to apologise, very deeply, for my behaviour when we last met. I hope very much that you will forgive me, if you can. I gave way to a sudden temptation, I'm afraid. You defied me and—'

'And you decided to punish me for it!' She raised her chin defiantly.

'No! How can you think that? I—oh, I've no excuse! But I shall have no peace of mind until you say I am forgiven.' He came close, taking her hand in his as he looked down into her eyes. 'Will you not trust me a little? You know I shall never give your secret away, it will be safe with me for ever. Why are you here and why must you work like this?'

The impulse to tell him was strong, so strong that for a moment she weakened. Then something made her draw back and she said slowly, not looking at him,

'You are right, Annie Fisher is the name I choose to use. I told you that I am untrained and this is work I can do and I am quite content with it. Please don't ask me to say any more, for I am afraid I must refuse.' She released her hand and, picking up the skirt of her print dress, she turned back. 'It is time to collect the children for their tea.'

He did not speak on the way back, but she was aware of his eyes resting on her speculatively. He was intrigued. Was that all? *Was* his interest something more than that? His presence disturbed her in a manner that both excited and dismayed her.

Thomas was waiting with the children. 'I've found the spot for the picnic,' he announced. 'There's a field behind the farmhouse and a swing for the children. You bring the rug, Giles, and Mark can carry the cushions and I'll take the tea-basket. We've been give some lardy cake and I'm hungry.'

He showed no surprise that the children's nurse should have strolled off with his friend. Probably he had not even noticed. She glanced at him and met his rather disturbingly perceptive blue eyes. No, Thomas Craig was not unaware of what went on around him. Not, of course, that his opinion was of any importance to her.

After they had finished tea, Thomas looked up and said,

'It's your turn to give the children a swing, Alex. I'll help pack up these tea-things.'

'Please don't bother,' Vicky said swiftly, 'I can easily do it.'

He watched Alex go off with the boys before turning to look at her.

'I've no doubt you can. But I want to say something to you and this is a good opportunity to do it.'

'Say something to me?' She stared at him indignantly. Was she to be scolded for taking a walk with Alex?

'Yes.' He continued to look at her and something cool in his eyes made her instinctively stiffen. 'Don't get involved with Alex Beaumont.' He said it deliberately, holding her gaze. 'And don't fall in love with him.'

He got to his feet and strolled away, leaving her to stare after him, furious—and uneasy.

CHAPTER
SIX

THE drive home was without interest for Vicky. She paid
no attention to the touch of autumn's paint-brush on
beech and oak and the drifting gold of birch leaves. The
children's chatter went unheeded. She was seeing Alex's
intent face and feeling the touch of his hand on hers—
and hearing Thomas's astonishing, shameless warning
about his friend.

Anger was uppermost in her feelings, anger against
the man to whom she had taken a dislike and who had no
right to speak to her as he had spoken. A sudden idea
made her anger glow afresh; did Thomas think she was
trying to lure Alex into marriage—or a sordid liaison?
Was his only aim that of protecting his friend from the
wiles of a nursemaid who was not what she seemed?

Their arrival at the house broke into her highly uncomfortable thoughts and the rest of the evening was
busy. Sue had the evening off to visit her mother, or so
she said, although Vicky had a suspicion it was James's
evening off also.

The children were tired and inclined to be naughty
after their day out. Giles was disappointed that Thomas
and Alex had not ridden back with them, but had set off
across the country at a rousing gallop.

'I think Thomas might have come home with us,' he
grumbled. 'I like Thomas, don't you, Annie?'

'No, I do not!' She spoke hotly and saw Giles's startled
eyes as he turned from the wash-basin to stare at her.

'Then you're *naughty*,' he said severely. 'He's nice. Mark and I think he's *very* nice.'

'It's wicked to say you hate people,' Mark remarked.

'I didn't say I hated him.' But perhaps she did hate him now for his unwarranted, impertinent and wholly unjustifiable innuendo about Alex.

'Don't get involved . . . don't fall in love . . .' The words kept her awake for a long time, thwarting all attempts to drown them in sleep. Why should he think such a thing possible? He had seen her with Alex only a few times. But if he had seen them that evening . . . She grew hot, then cold. If he had seen Alex kiss her he might well think she had invited it. Whatever he thought, she would never forgive him! He was a prying creature full of evil suspicions.

Preparations for visitors brought the household into a bustle of activity as hitherto unused bedrooms and dressing-rooms were dusted, swept and polished, curtains and bed hangings laundered and windows cleaned. The house was to be full for the coming ball, and there was a continuous coming and going of maids, housemen, footmen and gardeners, the latter staggering under potted palms and ferns for the hall and the long ballroom.

The famous Spode dinner-service with the Falconer arms was brought out from cupboards and crystal glass was rinsed in vinegar and polished to a high shine.

The general excitement affected the children and the boys refused to attend to their studies. Even Lucy, usually so placid, declared she would not drink her milk unless she was allowed to see what was going on. Vicky persuaded the housekeeper to take them all on a tour of the bedrooms with their velvet curtains, draped dressing-tables, marble-topped wash hand-stands complete with floral china basin, jug, soap-holder and toothbrush vase. Charming little rosewood writing tables were equipped with crested writing paper and envelopes, pen

and ink and, as a gentle hint, a railway timetable. Beds
had satin or lace spreads under which lay linen sheets
and pillow cases threaded with satin ribbon and fleecy-
soft blankets.

'I'll warrant the Queen don't have no better,' Sue
remarked proudly. 'Come away from that wash stand,
Master Giles.'

'I'm only smelling the soap,' Giles said. 'It smells like
lilies.'

'Straight from Bond Street, London,' Sue whispered,
'and it's *that* expensive. Housekeeper takes the bits the
visitors leave. Trust her!'

As the days passed, Vicky too became affected by the
atmosphere of anticipation and excitement. The nursery
was cut off from most of the activity in the rest of the
house, but Sue got news from James and retailed it to
Vicky.

Vicky was taking the children for a walk in the cool
autumn sunshine when they saw the first arrivals. Two
motor cars drove up with much snorting and puffing, and
shortly afterwards the Falconer carriage brought more
guests from the station, followed by Obediah Dumble
and the wagon bringing the luggage.

'There's that Miss Grange and her mother,' Mark
said. 'Why do they come here again?'

Vicky thought she knew. Alex Beaumont was still at
Wellbury Court, although she had not seen him since the
farm picnic. That, no doubt, was the magnet that drew
pretty, wealthy Effie Grange back to Devonshire. Did
Alex like her? He certainly appeared to pay her some
attention, but James had confided to Sue that 'she
hasn't got Mr Beaumont hooked yet, she hasn't' a remark which Vicky was honest enough to admit pleased
her.

That evening she let the children watch with her from
the hall gallery as the guests went in to dinner. Light

from the great gas chandeliers fell upon rich silks and
satins and taffetas, on creamy arms and necks adorned
with jewels, on bouffant hair trimmed with feathers or
flowers as the company, each woman on the arm of her
partner, swept across the hall to the dining-room which
had two liveried footmen flanking the door.

The light treble of the women's voices played counter-
point to the men's baritone and, as she watched, Vicky
was seized with a sudden longing to be one of the
beautifully gowned, self-confident women below. To let
her hand rest lightly on Alex Beaumont's arm while she
smiled up into his dark, amused eyes, to flirt with him,
tease him, tempt him, pretend indifference, scold him
for too ardent compliments—and then forgive him!

She saw him, disturbingly attractive, bending his head
to catch Effie Grange's remark. The heiress looked
charming in pink crêpe-de-chine beaded in silver and her
face was happy and animated.

'There's Thomas,' Mark said loudly.

'You oughtn't to call him that,' Lucy rebuked him,
'he's Mr Craig.'

'He said I could call him Thomas,' Mark told her
loftily.

Thomas heard. He looked up and grinned at three
small heads behind the banisters. Vicky drew back
abruptly. She had no desire to meet his cool blue eyes
again.

'I wish he would come up and talk to us,' Giles sighed.
'Do we have to go to bed straight away, Annie? I'm not a
bit sleepy.'

She thought it best to allow them a little time to settle
down after the excitement. Sue had slipped off to snatch
a word with James. Vicky was reading out *Robinson
Crusoe* when the door opened and looking up she met
Alex's eyes.

The boys made for him, demanding to know what

there had been for dinner and what the visitors were doing now.

'The ladies have deserted us,' he told them, smiling down into Vicky's eyes. 'I felt too lonely to stay.'

'There aren't any ladies here,' Mark pointed out. 'Annie isn't a lady, she's a nurse. Were there any sugared almonds? They're my *favourite* things.'

'I believe so, but they aren't good for young people. Isn't that so, Nurse Annie?'

'Possibly, Mr Beaumont.' She had recovered from the surprise of seeing him and she rose, slim and graceful despite the cotton dress with its bunchy skirt and starched apron. 'I'm afraid it is bedtime now. They have already stayed up too late.'

He made no protest as she shepherded them out of the room. When she returned he had gone, but on the table lay three little packets marked 'Giles', 'Mark', and 'Lucy'. A peep inside showed her the delectable pink and white sugared almonds that were Mark's 'favourite things'.

He had taken the trouble to bring the little treat to the nursery, hiding it until the children were in bed. How kind and thoughtful of him! Somehow she had not imagined his making such a gesture. She was standing looking down at the little packets when Sue entered.

'Eh, they're there, just as he said. The children'll be right happy tomorrow when they see them. It isn't often a gentleman takes thought of little 'uns like that,' she nodded at the table.

'It certainly was very kind of Mr Beaumont,' Vicky agreed.

'Laws, it wasn't he, 'twas Mr Craig as brought them. I met him outside and he said to hide them till after breakfast lest they make themselves sick.' She swept up the packets and put them in a cupboard while Vicky stared at her. Thomas again! Why did he have to intrude into everything?

'Thank goodness I wasn't here when he came,' she thought crossly, and refused to acknowledge her ill-temper was largely because it had not been Alex who had thought of the children.

A strange restlessness gripped her next morning. Sue noticed it and after breakfast, said,

'You hasn't had a day off since you came, Annie. You're 'titled to it, you know. You could do a bit of shopping in Exeter if someone was driving in.'

A day off! That was what she needed, Vicky decided. To get away from the house—and her own thoughts. When Lady Falconer paid an unexpected visit to the nursery, the request was made and granted.

'You may find one of the grooms driving into town,' Lady Falconer told her. 'I believe the shops are quite good there. You must not be late coming back, of course. Tomorrow I wish the children to come down after tea, just for a quarter of an hour. You know, Lucy is growing so fast I think she needs some new dresses. I shall tell the housekeeper to get Miss Grindly to come, she is an excellent dressmaker.'

'She sticks pins into me,' Lucy complained. 'Can I have a blue dress with lace on it, Mama?'

'Perhaps—I don't know. I shall leave it to Miss Grindly. Oh dear,' she brushed a slim hand across her brow, 'really, I sometimes wonder why we planned this ball! *So* much to see to and so many problems . . . People can be so inconsiderate. There is no peace or quiet anywhere in the house!'

'You will find the nursery peaceful, my lady,' Vicky remarked, 'like the eye of a storm.'

Lady Falconer looked at her in sudden interest. 'What a strange little person you are, Annie. Your manners and looks are so different that one could almost think . . .

I shall give you some money to buy a dress for the afternoon, I don't care for that print thing, and you need not wear an apron when you bring the children downstairs. I think I can rely on you to get something suitable, grey or brown of course, and for goodness' sake, buy a more becoming cap.' She got up, smoothing down the lace sleeves of her gown. 'You are really quite pretty, Annie, and you have the *strangest* eyes. No, Lucy dear, Mama cannot stay, she is *very* busy now she has so many visitors.'

As soon as Lady Falconer had left, Vicky ran down to the stableyard where she found Obediah Dumble polishing a piece of harness while smoking a noisome pipe.

He removed the pipe to answer her query. 'Oh aye, I'll be taking the wagon into town this afternoon. You'll have an hour afore I starts back.'

'Well, that will have to do,' she said, a little ruefully, 'thank you, Dumble.'

'I'll be setting out around half-past two—' Dumble's eyes went past her and he bobbed his head. 'Morning, Mr Beaumont. You'll want Blackie I 'spect. It's a fine morning for riding.'

Vicky turned, startled. She had not heard his step on the cobbles.

Alex shook his head. 'I'm driving today, Dumble,' he said easily. 'Can I have the pony trap? I want to go into Exeter.'

'You'll not be taking your motor car, sir?'

'No. It's a fine day and I've a fancy to take the trap.' He turned to Vicky. 'I believe I heard you say you wished to go into the town, Nurse? I shall be driving in shortly and not returning until, possibly, four o'clock, which will give you time to shop.'

She managed to repress her excitement and say calmly: 'Thank you, sir, I would be grateful as I have several things to do and I do not yet know my way about the town. When shall I be ready?'

He glanced at his watch. 'In half an hour.'

She slipped away, her eyes sparkling. The gods were surely on her side to have brought Alex into the yard at just that moment. Yet a faint unease took away some of her pleasure. Would Lady Falconer approve of her nurse driving alone with one of her guests, a most attractive bachelor? Something told her it would *not* be thought at all suitable and she ought to wait and go with Dumble in the wagon. The thought depressed her, but not for long.

'I could not possibly buy a dress in an hour,' she told herself. 'And Lady Falconer has ordered me to get it and wear it tomorrow. I do not believe she will ever know I have gone with him. *He* won't tell her—and he will drive down the back avenue so we shan't be seen.'

Dumble knew, of course, but somehow she did not think the man would gossip.

She gave Sue instructions to take the children in the park after luncheon, and hurried to put on her horrid brown coat and straw hat. Down in the stable yard she found Dumble rubbing up the woodwork of a neat little pony trap. When she began to explain her need for a longer time in town, he nodded somewhat brusquely.

'I have been told to do some shopping by Lady Falconer,' she said. 'I don't think she will find it strange if I accept the chance to have more time in the town. But—'

''Tis no business of mine,' he told her. 'I doesn't go talking of what don't concern me, if that's what you're thinking.'

It *was* what she had been thinking and his obvious disapproval did not please her. But she forgot him and his disapproval when Alex came into the yard. He helped her into the trap, and then got in, taking up the reins as he remarked,

'That's a smart little animal, Dumble. We'll make short work of the miles with him.'

As she had guessed, he turned the pony into the side avenue, remarking it was shorter and would save time.

'And be out of sight of the house,' she said demurely.

He glanced at her, his eyes full of laughter. 'As you so rightly say, Miss Annie Fisher, away from prying eyes. Are you indeed being very rash, to drive with me?'

'Well, I think it would be thought unusual—in fact, quite unsuitable, and I'd much rather no one *did* see us,' she said frankly.

'Dumble saw us.'

'He says he doesn't talk of what does not concern him.'

'An estimable character, our Dumble. His discretion shall be rewarded.'

The day had all the mellow warmth of autumn, sharpened occasionally by a refreshing wind that sent down a shower of gold and tawny leaves as it swept through the trees lining the avenue. Vicky sat back, her eyes bright with pleasure, prepared to enjoy herself to the utmost. A rabbit darted across their path. A pheasant strutted in a field, showing off his jewel colours. Autumn flowers blazed in the garden of the cottage at the end of the avenue where a dog barked and raced beside them until they swung out into the Exeter road.

'You are very silent, Miss Annie,' Alex's voice broke into her musings.

'I was thinking what a perfect day it is, and what a beautiful estate Sir Charles and Lady Falconer have.'

'Yes, it's a fine place. Old Falconer looked after it well, but Charles is somewhat lazy about improvements.'

'Such as repairing the balcony on the west side.'

He looked up sharply. 'How did you know that?'

'I was downstairs when Sir Charles mentioned it. You had been looking at it and he didn't appear very interested in your report.'

'Oh, that's Charles, he can't be bothered.'

'Is the balcony really unsafe?'

'Possibly. Tell me, what do you propose to do when we reach town?'

'I have to buy a dress and that will take time. And I would like to look at some shops.' She did not mention her determination to replace the depressing underclothes and nightgowns with something better. Nurse Brodmin would not have approved, but luckily she no longer ruled the Falconer nursery.

The journey was all too short for Vicky. Alex was a charming companion, lively and interesting in his conversation and treating her quite as if she had been one of the visitors at Wellbury Court. Glancing at him from under her lashes, she wondered if he was indeed the same man who had once behaved in so ungentlemanly a fashion. She felt her face grow warm at the memory of his kiss and turned her head, ostensibly to observe the outskirts of the town they were entering. No, she did not really know him; was that part of his fascination for her? Or was she drawn to him for a deeper, more disturbing reason? A feather touch of fear made her wonder if she were playing a dangerous game and where it would end.

'I shall put up the trap at the George,' Alex said. 'They give you quite a decent luncheon there. You must be hungry. Nursery breakfast is probably early.'

'I shall find a café—' she began, but he broke in saying,

'You are having luncheon with me at the George, I insist. I know what women have in cafés, weak tea and buns. You are not a weak-tea-and-bun young woman.'

She laughed. 'I suppose that is a compliment. But I

really cannot possibly have luncheon with you, someone might see me.'

'No one will be in town from Wellbury Court today except Dumble,' he said, turning the pony in the entrance to the George's stableyard, 'and I very much doubt if he patronises the George. Do not deny me the pleasure of your company, Miss Annie. Do not forget I have yet to receive assurance that I am forgiven for what was most reprehensible behaviour, I fear.'

Her grey eyes were amused as she looked at him. 'Can I be assured you truly regret your behaviour, Mr Beaumont?'

'No, by heavens, I don't!' He threw the reins to the stable boy and helped her out of the trap. 'Come, I'll be teased no longer. I am determined to know your secret, little Miss Nurse. I may not get such a chance as this again.'

She threw all caution to the winds as she went with him into the inn, which had once been a coaching inn. As he had said, it was unlikely anyone who knew her would be there, and if they were, she did not care! Today she was Victoria Lynton, although she might not reveal that just yet to the man who preceded her into the oak-beamed dining-room.

The food, after the plain nursery fare, was delicious and she enjoyed it heartily. Alex did not talk much, but his eyes were often on her and she saw the speculation in them and was amused.

When he demanded the reason for her smile, she finished the last spoonful of raspberry tart before answering.

'I was thinking how very unlike you and your friend, Thomas Craig, are.'

He looked surprised. 'Thomas? We've known each other for years, first at Eton and then at Pembroke. He was rather a swot and did better than I. He went into the law, a profession I should find deadly boring. He does pretty well, I'm told, doesn't have to chase up work, you know. What made you think of him?'

'I just wondered what you had in common, that is all.'

'Actually very little,' he admitted, leaning back in his chair. 'He often pops up in houses where I'm staying, he's a popular visitor, doesn't flirt with the women or drink too much of his host's claret.'

'Is he . . .' she hesitated, '. . . a very *great* friend?'

He eyed her thoughtfully. 'Why, do you think he might not be a very great friend?'

'I—just wondered,' she murmured. What would Alex think if he knew that Thomas had warned her against him? Would he be angry? Amused? She decided not to risk telling him. 'I haven't time for any coffee, I must find the shops. Thank you for a very delightful lunch, Mr Beaumont. At what time shall I meet you here?'

She had to repeat the question. Alex had risen and was standing staring down at the table, apparently deep in thought. He gave a start and looked up to say,

'Thank you for giving me the pleasure of your company. I plan to start back at four o'clock. Does that suit you?'

She assured him it did and, leaving him, went off to seek some shop where she could find something that would be pretty, but not of course *too* pretty, in grey. Brown did not suit her.

Luck was with her. A dress of dove-grey ribbed silk, with an under-blouse of tucked cream net, fitted her slim figure perfectly.

'You should wear something green with it, Miss,' the saleswoman said, 'because of your eyes, if you'll excuse me. I could put a little ruching of green velvet at the neckline . . .'

Vicky agreed recklessly. A spirit of rebellion had seized her and she bought delicate linen underclothes,

ribbon-run nightgowns and a pair of bronze slippers.
The gay little butterfly cap was meant to be the last of her
purchases, but when she saw a silver-grey dust-coat of
elegant cut and a little bonnet that was both demure and
extremely becoming, she could not resist them. Away
with the brown holland horror and straw hat! As head
nurse surely it was her duty to look well dressed.

'As long as I don't appear in anything but grey or
brown,' she thought. '*How* I shall enjoy wearing pretty
colours again.'

And how much prettier I shall look, was her thought.
Alex will see . . . But would Alex be there when she
shed her protective colouring? The end of her escapade
was still out of sight. It *was* possible that Alex was
amusing himself in a situation he found piquant. She was
a mystery he wished to solve and her evasion served to
strengthen his wish. Once she had revealed who she was,
would he lose interest? Would he turn his attention to
pretty Effie Grange who had such an enticing fortune?

The thought was still in her mind when she reached
the entrance to the inn stableyard. To her dismay, she
saw Effie Grange in lively conversation with Alex.

'It was a sudden whim,' she was saying, tilting her
head to look up at him. 'The others went off to see some
old church and I thought I would like to do a little
shopping in town with old Lady French. Lady Falconer
offered us the Daimler, but Lady French does not care
for motors so we came in the Victoria. What are you
doing here, Alex?'

'Oh, I simply wanted a book and some writing things,'
he saw Vicky hesitating behind Effie, 'and I was able to
give Lady Falconer's nurse a lift into town in the pony
trap.'

'You must come back with us, Alex,' Effie declared
gaily. 'I refuse to take no for an answer. I'm sure nurse
can drive herself back in the trap, that pony is very

well-behaved, I know.' She turned to Vicky with a smile. 'Isn't that so, Nurse?'

'Yes, Miss Grange, I can drive a trap.' Vicky shot a swift glance at Alex and caught the flash of irritation in his eyes. 'It was very kind of Mr Beaumont to drive me in.'

'But not terribly wise,' Effie laughed lightly. 'If Lady Falconer knew you had driven Nurse in—but we shan't tell her. The carriage is in the next street and Lady French is waiting. Come along, Alex, I shall tell you about the new arrivals who came after luncheon.'

'You know, I really think I ought to drive the trap back . . .' his eyes went to Vicky who gave an almost imperceptible shake of her head. 'I'm not sure Nurse Fisher can—'

'I have often driven a pony trap, Mr Beaumont,' Vicky said with a serenity she was far from feeling. What unfortunate chance had brought Effie Grange on the scene just at this moment! 'I can manage perfectly, if you will be kind enough to tell the boy to harness the pony.'

Effie accompanied them into the yard, giving Alex no chance to speak to Vicky. As he handed her the reins he began to say something under his breath, but Effie broke in, saying,

'We really must hurry, Alex, the old lady gets impatient if she's kept waiting.'

The pony behaved excellently and there was little traffic on the road. Sunlight still mellowed the countryside, making the glimpses of red Devon earth glow rosily. But all joy in the day was gone for Vicky. She had planned to reveal a little more of the truth about herself to Alex on the drive back, and to discover something more about his false friend, Thomas—and perhaps to agree to the meeting she was certain he would suggest. And now Alex was lolling in the carriage being gently flattered and made much of by Effie. Her thoughts did nothing to cheer her. Alex had gone off rather too lightly with Effie, she considered. He had made no really serious attempt to refuse her offer—no, her *demand* that he accompany her back to Wellbury Court. The day that had begun so excitingly had ended in disappointment.

'Well, I hope that is the last uncomfortable thing to happen to me,' she thought as, having left the pony and trap with the stable boy, she went into the house. 'First Thomas's positive *insolence*, and now *this*.'

But she was destined to suffer one more highly uncomfortable, not to say disastrous stroke of ill-luck when she came out onto the landing on the floor below the nursery and found herself looking into the incredulous and horrified eyes of her sister Maud.

CHAPTER
SEVEN

For a second Vicky could not believe her eyes. What was Maud doing in Wellbury Court, and how was she to explain her own presence in the house as nurse to the Falconer children? Vicky's mind, ever at its most fertile in emergencies, worked furiously, while her sister struggled to find words to express her amazement.

'*Vicky!* Why are you here? Why are you dressed like that? I thought you were staying in Norfolk with Great-Aunt Matilda!'

'Hush, Maud. I'll explain. Where is your room?'

'Along the passage—'

'We'll go there so we can talk.' She took Maud's arm and firmly piloted her to her bedroom where she shut and locked the door and then turned to face her bewildered sister.

'First of all, Maud, tell me why *you* are here. You were left with Flora to finish the season.'

'It's finished. Flora has gone to Scotland, but I didn't really wish to go and luckily for me, some friends I had made recently—a Lady Grange and her sweet daughter—arranged for me to be included in an invitation to visit the Falconers and attend the ball being given here. It sounded too deevy! But *you* explain why you are here, Vicky. I'm sure Mama and Father think—'

'Think I am vegetating in Norfolk,' Vicky agreed, seating herself in a chair. 'But I decided I didn't want to go, you see. I should have been horribly bored. I wanted to see life from a different standpoint, so I've taken the position of nurse to Lady Falconer's children and I find it *most* interesting and enjoyable, I assure you.' She began to laugh. 'Oh Maud, do look less appalled! I'm only doing it for a short while, I have no intention of making it my life's work. But I did want to do some sort of work, and being a nurse is highly respectable, you must admit.'

'But Mama will be *dreadfully* shocked and upset!' Maud's huge blue eyes were fixed on her errant sister in fascinated horror.

'Oh no, because she need never know. I shall leave here before Mama and Father return—and probably visit Aunt Matilda.'

'*She* will tell Mama you have not been with her the whole time.'

'You know, I wonder if she will.' Vicky looked out of the window, her eyes thoughtful. 'I believe she will understand rather better than anyone. I don't think she would give me away.' She swung around. 'And *you* are not going to give me away, Maud dear. I know you think I'm being quite mad, but you cannot say I am disgracing the family, or being immoral—'

'Oh no, Vicky, of course you would not do anything really *wrong*, at least . . .' Maud hesitated, sadly bewildered, 'I suppose it *is* wrong to tell lies, and pretend to be a servant.'

'Head nurse,' Vicky corrected her. 'Now Maud, listen. I am Annie Fisher and you have never seen me before. Your sister Vicky is bringing comfort and light into the life of her great-aunt in Norfolk. You know nothing of all this, so you cannot be blamed if there is trouble later.'

'But—'

Vicky rose and advanced upon her wavering sister.

'If you give me away, Maud, I promise you I *shall* do something highly immoral!'

'Oh Vicky! You have always had such *strange* notions.

I fear you are quite *wild* sometimes. I don't understand you; I would *never* want to be a—a nurse.'

'You will never need to be one, my dear. When you are married to Archie Burnley he will provide you with all the nurses you want. By the way, has he proposed yet?'

Maud's rosy face gave Vicky her answer. 'Oh Vicky, he has said he—he loves me and wants me to marry him! Of course we are keeping it a *complete* secret, Archie will have to speak to Father before there can be an official engagement.'

Vicky kissed her warmly. 'Dear Maud, I'm so delighted, and I know you will be very happy. I'll keep your secret and you will keep mine.'

'I suppose I will have to,' Maud sighed. 'But I shall feel guilty. I don't think Archie will approve.'

'I'm sure he won't,' Vicky agreed, 'so don't make the poor man unhappy by telling him what a peculiar sister-in-law he will have. Now I must go to the nursery. I've been shopping in Exeter, I got a drive in with one of the visitors, a Mr Alex Beaumont.'

'Alex Beaumont? That is the man poor Effie likes so much,' Maud exclaimed as Vicky went to the door.

With her hand on the door handle, Vicky turned. 'Why *poor* Effie? She's an heiress.'

'Oh yes she is, but she is rather dreadfully fond of Alex and now her mother won't let her see him—although if he is here, she will have to see him, won't she? It will be frightfully awkward for Effie, I fear.'

'But I thought Lady Grange liked him. In fact, encouraged his attentions to her daughter.'

'Oh that was before she discovered he . . .' Maud's voice sank to a shocked whisper, '. . . he *gambled*! Effie told me all about it.' She stared at Vicky in dismay. 'Oh dear! I promised I would not tell anyone.'

'You have only told Annie Fisher who will soon cease

to exist,' Vicky told her cheerfully, 'so you are quite safe. I shall see you tomorrow when I bring the children down to the drawing-room, but you are not to see me, remember.'

'Very well,' her sister sighed. 'You are a funny girl.'

'Who likes doing funny things. But you are a faithful sister who will not give me away, bless you.'

Vicky left the room smiling. Maud, she knew, would hold her tongue even though she disapproved. She was safe for the time being. Later, she would find a moment to get family news from Maud and find out when her parents were expected home.

A thought struck her. What would Lady Grange's reactions be when she knew her daughter had driven back from town in company with the man she had been forbidden to see? A man who was a gambler.

'I wonder if he *is*,' she thought as she went to the nursery. 'Most men gamble in one way or another, horses, cards or rash speculations. I expect Effie's mother thinks Alex might gamble away her daughter's fortune.'

She had no time to think further as the children claimed her attention with accounts of how they had spent their day. One of the guests, a young man whose hobby appeared to be photography, had been taking photographs of the house, gardens and children.

'We had to pretend to be playing,' Giles said, 'not stand still and smile as we do when Mama takes us to the man in London.'

'He said Lucy was *pretty*,' Mark said, stating a fact he obviously found difficult to believe. He studied his sister sternly. 'I expect he can't see very well.'

As she went about her duties, Vicky continued to think about Alex and to wonder if indeed he had intended to drive into the town or if, as she suspected, he had heard her asking Dumble for a lift. The latter would mean he was willing to give up a morning's riding in the park for the pleasure of being with her, and the knowledge made her heart leap and sent a glow to her cheeks—and increased the odd twinges of uneasiness that she could not quite suppress when she thought of his growing interest in her and her own reaction to it.

Was she liking him too much? Or was he just part of the amusing but short break-away from her normal life? Would she have come to Wellbury Court if she had never seen Alex and heard his words that evening? Was her uneasiness due to the possibility that Alex, a carefree bachelor determined to remain heartwhole, was merely intrigued with the situation?

A polite babel of voices greeted her when she entered the drawing-room next afternoon with the children. She stood discreetly in the deep window embrasure and watched the scene with interest, wondering if she would recognise anyone. Old Lady French had visited her mother's at-home, but she would never recognise the demure figure in the pretty grey and cream dress and butterfly cap. The others, except for Maud, were strangers to her, much to her relief. The women in their pretty, light, frilly dresses looked like a display of hothouse flowers. Alex stood with a group of men at the far end of the room. As he saw the children, he moved away and came to stand near Effie Grange who greeted him with a smile.

The children were talking to a tall, thin young man with a blond moustache. Vicky heard him say,

'Tomorrow morning, if the sun shines. I will meet you in the Italian garden, it will make an excellent background, I think.'

'When can we see our photographs?' Giles asked.

'Yes,' Effie turned to the young man with a smile, 'when are we to observe a specimen of your art, Mr Brett? I quite dote on artistic photographs.'

'Sir Charles has kindly put a dark-room at my disposal, so I can develop plates,' Mr Brett told her importantly. 'It is not all done in a minute, I can assure you, Miss Grange.'

'Oh, do let us have a group photograph of the house-party,' Lady Falconer exclaimed, 'sitting on the front steps.'

'Ladies in the front looking angelic and men at the back looking fierce, with dogs lying at their feet,' Alex suggested lazily.

Lady Grange was frowning. 'Effie, come over here, I want you to tell Miss Greyson where you buy your embroidery silk.'

Her daughter rose with heightened colour and moved away from Alex. Vicky felt sorry for the girl as she caught the quick glances exchanged between the other visitors. If she was truly in love with Alex . . . But who could fail to be attracted by his handsome looks and compelling charm? He had not looked at Vicky since she had entered the room and she knew she ought to be grateful, but perversely she was not. Once again she felt the wish to be herself, the last Miss Lynton, in a Paris gown and at home among the beautifully dressed women and well-mannered men chatting so easily and lightly in the long, charmingly furnished room with its soft grey walls and rose curtains that framed views of smooth lawns and noble stands of trees. Was it because of Alex? She sighed—and heard Thomas Craig say,

'Don't envy them, they aren't all as carefree as they appear.'

She turned with a start and met his eyes, cool and speculative as they rested on her.

'I assure you I was not envying anyone,' she said coldly, and added, albeit reluctantly, '—sir.'

He grinned. 'You know, I prefer "Mr Craig" on the whole. May I congratulate you on your very attractive dress? A great improvement on that bunchy print thing.'

She stared at him indignantly. 'No, you may not! It is most improper for you to be talking to me at all, Mr Craig.'

'Oh, I've done my social duty, handing around sandwiches and cakes, although the footman does it much better than I do. Tell me, did you enjoy your visit to Exeter?' She knew he was amused at the colour that flew to her face and she hated him for it. 'Can I say how well you handle a pony trap, Miss Annie. I was in the park and saw you return,' he added, forestalling her question.

'How did you know—'

'Where you had been? Miss Grange mentioned meeting you. I don't think you would have thought of taking the trap out alone, so someone must have driven you in and deserted you for, shall we suppose, some greater attraction.'

Really he was quite insufferable! How dare he speak to her like this! Vicky glared at him and heard him say thoughtfully,

'You know, your eyes go quite green when you lose your temper.'

'I have *not* lost my temper.'

'Oh yes you have, Miss Annie Fisher. And you are busy hating me because I warned you against Alex Beaumont.'

She caught her breath and glanced swiftly around her, but luckily no one seemed to have noticed them as they stood in the window, half hidden by a curtain.

'And you are supposed to be his *friend*,' she said furiously.

'I've known Alex for a long time,' he spoke deliberately, his eyes holding hers. 'He's one of the most popular and charming fellows I know—and that, Miss Annie, makes him dangerous.'

'To me?' she demanded. 'Do you think I am—am trying to capture his attention?'

'I think you are trying to fall in love with him, and I strongly advise you not to.' The dispassionate expression on his strong, blunt features was belied by a glint of laughter deep in his eyes as he watched her eyes blaze.

'How dare you! You are grossly impertinent . . .' she was shocked into silence by her sudden, primitive desire to hit him.

'I shouldn't, you know,' he said gently, 'it might cause a slight sensation—and some enquiry into who you really are, Miss Annie Fisher.' He walked away, unruffled, stolid—and hateful.

She waited until she had control of her feelings, feelings that were for the moment wholly concerned with Thomas Craig and his monstrous accusation. She saw Lady Falconer beckoning and went forward to collect the children and, with deep relief, take them back to the nursery.

The children's chatter and Sue's accounts of what James had told her about the trouble between the cook and the butler, passed over her head. She was too angry with Thomas, and too uneasy. She had given herself away to him; no nurse would have spoken as she had to him. He knew she was not what she seemed. Would he say something to Lady Falconer and would she be dismissed?

The unexpected appearance of her sister Maud put an end to her most unpleasant musings.

'Lady Falconer said I might come and say goodnight to the children,' Maud said uncertainly, glancing at Sue. 'Dear little Lucy is a sweet child.'

'Certainly, Miss Lynton.' Vicky turned to Sue. 'Please ask the kitchen to give Miss Lucy cocoa for breakfast, she dislikes milk.' When the girl had gone, she swung

around on Maud. 'Well, did I look the part this afternoon?'

'Oh yes, I hardly noticed you hiding in the window.
But Vicky, I really think you ought—'

'Please, Maud dear, stop thinking about me and
instead give me news of the family.'

Apparently Sir Andrew and Lady Lynton were to
remain in the States for another two weeks and then
they were to visit Boston where they would stay with
Harriet's future in-laws.

'So they won't be home until about the end of
October,' Vicky murmured. 'What are your plans?'

Maud said she was returning to London after the ball
as her sister would be back from Scotland by then and
Lord Burnley back from a duty visit to his parents in
Norfolk.

Vicky's slender brows rose. 'Norfolk? Let us hope he
won't meet Aunt Matilda. You will have to think of
some explanation of my not being with her if he does,
Maud.'

'Oh dear, I'm so poor at explanations,' Maud sighed.

'Don't worry,' Vicky said, 'I never do—at least, not
often. What is happening with Effie and Alex? Has
her mother relented? Is the girl really serious about
him?'

'Oh, I think so. She is very upset, of course. Her
mother would take her away if she wasn't afraid of
offending Lady Falconer. Effie has been such *great*
friends with Alex, they have met at so many house-
parties. Effie was staying with the McDonaldsons in Fife
that time some jewels were stolen and it was all so
exciting, she said, and she and Alex went around looking
for clues and the police came and everyone was questioned, but nothing was ever discovered.'

'Brought together by crime,' Vicky suggested, 'quite
romantic. Perhaps Alex is a gentleman burglar with a

useful entrée into the best houses and *he* stole the jewels.'

'Good gracious, what a dreadful idea!' Maud was plainly shocked. 'Anyway, there were lots of other men there, though of course none of them could *possibly* have been burglars.'

'A pity, it was an intriguing thought. Who else was in the house-party?'

'Oh, the usual crowd, you know. Lady French and the Bailey girls, Lord Nordham, Mr Thomas Craig and that Mr Brett who is so mad on photography and a man who had explored in Africa and was nearly eaten by savages. I must go now. *Please* don't do anything dreadful, will you? Goodnight, Vicky.'

When her sister had gone, Vicky wandered restlessly around the room, picking up a toy here, replacing a book there, plumping up the cushion in the basket chair. Would it be very dreadful to fall in love with Alex? He was attracted to her; possibly by now he was in love with her. His attentions to Effie were, she guessed, aimed at teasing her mother. Such a situation would amuse him.

'However, I am *not* going to think about him,' she told herself, and went to bed and, to her great annoyance, dreamed of Thomas Craig.

Both boys were at their bedroom window when Vicky went to call them next morning.

'It's going to be sunny and we can have our photographs taken by Mr Brett. I like him, he lets me look at his camera,' Mark said.

'You will have to do your lessons with your tutor, I'm afraid,' Vicky reminded him.

'No we won't,' Giles said, turning around. 'Mr Brett asked Mama to let us off lessons if the day was fine. We're to go to the Italian garden at half-past ten.'

'Then you had better wear a clean shirt and your best

suit, and see your hair is neat and your hands are clean,'
she warned him before going to wake Lucy and put out a
white embroidered dress and pink satin sash.

She was glad to have something to keep her mind off
yesterday's conversation with Thomas Craig. She was
irritated with herself for being so disturbed by his words.
Thomas, she told herself crossly, did not matter. He was
one of those insufferable creatures who must always be
interfering in people's lives.

The sun slid out from the light morning haze and
shone obligingly on the little Italian garden, making the
dew-drops on tree and shrub diamond-bright. The children played, chasing each other along the many formal
little paths until the arrival of the earnest Mr Brett
carrying his equipment.

'Against that stone wall, I think. Yes, the little girl's
dress will show up nicely. Boys, please look at your sister
and *not* at the camera. Nurse, could you arrange them a
trifle less—less stiffly?'

Vicky joined the restless children. 'Giles, leave Lucy's
hair alone. Mark, if you sat on the grass with Lucy beside
you, and Giles looking at something Lucy is holding—a
flower, I think.' She picked two asters from the flower
bed.

'Yes, yes, that is excellent,' Mr Brett agreed enthusiastically. 'The flowers add a charming touch of
nature. Now, *very* still, children . . .'

They remained reasonably still while he took several
more photographs and, when released, darted forward
to meet the man strolling into the garden. Thomas
Craig.

Vicky turned away abruptly. Was she forever to be
haunted by the wretched man? Why was he not out
riding, or playing billiards or reading the paper in the
smoking room like the other men?

She became aware of Mr Brett speaking to her.

'—if you would not mind, Nurse. Holding the little girl's hand, perhaps. I'd like you to look at the camera. Your eyes—what a pity I cannot show their most unusual colouring.'

'Silver when she is pleased with life,' Thomas remarked conversationally, 'a very dangerous green when she is angry.'

Mr Brett was too engrossed in adjusting the tripod to heed. He draped himself and the camera in a black cloth, his voice coming out muffled.

'Look up at Nurse, little girl . . . that's better. Could you get her to smile? She looks too serious.'

'Watch the birdies fly out of the camera, Lucy,' Vicky said and Lucy began to laugh.

'Silly, there aren't any birdies!'

'Splendid. Thank you, Nurse. I'll get busy developing these and you can see them later on in the week.'

'Come, boys,' Vicky said, 'we must go back.'

'Come with us, Thomas,' Giles begged, 'and play trains. We aren't having lessons today, isn't it a lark?'

'I'd be delighted—if your nurse agrees.'

'Oh Annie doesn't mind,' Mark said carelessly. 'She says she doesn't like you, but she'll let you come.'

Vicky walked out of the garden, holding Lucy's hand, her head high and a fervent wish in her heart that something or someone would free her of Thomas's most unwelcome presence.

Her wish was granted. As she left the garden she saw Alex ahead of her and he turned as he heard their steps. He was in riding clothes which suited his tall, athletic figure.

As they drew near, he said: 'Lucy, would you like to see the new kittens in the stable? There are five of them.'

'Oh, yes please!' Lucy's eyes brightened and she tugged at Vicky's hand. 'Do let us go and see them, Annie.'

Thomas and the boys had gone on ahead. Alex took Lucy's hand in his.

'Then we'll pay Mama cat a visit, shall we? Come along, both of you.'

In the yard, he called a stable lad to show Lucy the kittens, then turned to Vicky, his face suddenly serious and his dark eyes searching hers.

'Thomas seems to have a liking for visiting the nursery,' he said abruptly. 'Do you meet him often? Does he seek you out?'

She was taken aback for a minute. 'Well, he likes the children and, yes, he does sometimes come up to play with them.'

'He was talking to you yesterday, in the window. And he refused to ride this morning, he said he had other business. Was it with you?'

'Of course it wasn't. He just appeared while Mr Brett was taking studies of the children in the garden. Why on earth should he have any "business" with me?'

'That is what I wanted to discover. Look here, I don't like doing this. I have known Thomas for years, and, in spite of what I may . . . suspect, I dislike having to say it, but don't trust Thomas. Keep away from him. Don't have anything to do with him, for your own sake.'

His eyes held hers so she could not look away. She heard a horse move restlessly in a stable and Lucy's excited squeals from a shed. A ring dove cooed softly somewhere above them. Then the big stable clock chimed the hour and broke the spell.

'Don't get involved . . .' she said slowly. 'That was what he said about *you*.'

CHAPTER
EIGHT

For a second she seemed to be looking at the face of a stranger. A flash of something she could not define showed in his dark eyes as he stared at her. Then, as Lucy came running from the shed, all expression vanished, as if a shutter had come down over his face.

'There's a black kitten and a white one and a black-and-white one,' Lucy called breathlessly. 'Do come and see them, Annie.'

Alex spoke rapidly in a lowered voice. 'I've got to talk to you, it is important. Meet me tonight in the gardens. There's a small summer-house at the end of the long yew walk. I'll be there soon after half-past nine.'

'I—I'm not sure if I—'

'You *must* come. You've got to know something and there isn't time now. Nine-thirty in the summer-house.' He swung around and strode out of the yard.

The kittens had to be admired, and Lucy taken back to the nursery to join the boys before Vicky found time to try to sort out the tangled emotions Alex's words had aroused. To her great relief, Thomas had left.

She sat by the window, looking with unseeing eyes at the last of the dead leaves being blown across the lawns.

She was thinking: 'I don't think I should have told him about Thomas, I'm sure it was unwise. I wish I hadn't said anything. Alex looked so odd . . . *What* is it I must know, something about Thomas? But I don't wish to know more; I dislike the man, he's impertinent and interfering.'

Should she meet Alex? She had not said she would, but she knew her decision was already made. His charm had a magnetic quality that drew her to him. She was not truly in love with him, she assured herself, it was simply a light flirtation and part of her adventure. She determined to put all speculation out of her mind until she met him and discovered what it was he thought she must know.

The day seemed to drag and she was aware of being impatient with the children. When, at last, all three were in bed, she told Sue she had a headache and was going out for a short walk in the garden.

The wind was chill with a wintry bite in its sudden gusts as she hurried down the long dark yew walk to the little rustic summer-house. As she drew near she saw Alex standing in the entrance.

'Come inside, that wind is pretty beastly.'

Dead leaves, blown in by the wind, rustled under her feet as she followed him into the dim interior of the little house. She had come determined to be calm and self-possessed and to show none of the eagerness mixed with misgivings which she was feeling.

'If Lady Falconer knew of this I should be dismissed at once,' she said lightly. 'I am taking a risk, you know, and I mustn't stay long.'

'She will not know. Annie—no, I don't believe you are really Annie Fisher. What is your true name? Tell me, I promise not to divulge it.'

She hesitated. 'Vicky.'

'Just—Vicky?'

'Just Vicky,' she said firmly. 'What is it you have to tell me?'

For answer he moved nearer and caught her hand. In the darkness she could not see his expression, but she felt her heartbeat quicken at the pressure of his hand on hers.

'Are you sorry you've come, little Vicky of the sea-maiden's eyes?' he asked softly. 'Are you frightened?'

'Of course not, although I hope no one will see us,' she said firmly. She would not let him know how her heart was behaving. '*Why* did you ask me to meet you tonight?'

'Don't pretend you cannot guess one reason. I don't see you often enough,' his voice deepened, 'although in my thoughts and dreams you are there too much for my comfort, I fear.'

'You said you wanted to tell me something,' she said, a little breathlessly. It was the first time he had openly admitted her attraction for him. 'What is it, please? You know I cannot stay long.'

He released her hand and moved away. 'It's about Thomas. You said he warned you against me?'

'Well, yes,' she admitted uneasily. 'But probably he was not being serious. He may have thought—' she made her voice casual and a little amused '—that you might turn the head of an insignificant nursemaid. Of course, it was none of his business.'

'No, it was not,' he said sternly. 'But it is my business to tell you a little about Thomas. He's a barrister, you know, and has been rather successful, although some people have thought . . . He defended a receiver of stolen goods and got him off. It was considered quite a feat as the man was obviously guilty. Thomas was very clever over it. Naturally he had to do the best for his client and personally I didn't blame him.'

'But other people did?'

'Well, he had his living to make.'

'He seems to be able to take time off to pay visits,' she said slowly. 'I don't know much about the law as a profession, but I would have thought . . .'

'As a matter of fact, so would I. He appears to have plenty of leisure. He gets to all the big house-parties.'

'So do you,' she said, smiling.

'Ah, but I have a father who is uncommonly generous with my allowance. Thomas's father was in the army and there wasn't much for Thomas when he died.'

'I thought you were quite close friends.'

'Not really. Thomas disapproves of me, I fear. I don't criticise his way of life, but he frequently criticises mine. He did much the same trick at Eton, warning my friends I wasn't to be trusted. I had to have it out with him.'

'You mean, you fought him?'

'And whipped him rather badly, I'm afraid. I don't think he has ever quite forgotten – or forgiven. And now that your green eyes have caught his fancy, he is jealous—'

'*Jealous?* Oh no, that is impossible!' she declared vehemently. 'I hardly ever meet him. He comes to the nursery to see the children. I don't think he likes me.'

'Don't be too sure. Tell me, do you like him?'

'No, not now, and you are really quite wrong about his having any interest in me, I assure you.'

'I wonder. He wants to get me out of the way by warning you I'm a bad character. Vicky, you must not trust him. I know rather more than I've said about him. Promise me you won't have anything to do with him.'

'Of course I won't, because I will have no opportunity, even if I wanted to. Now I *must* go.'

'Not until you have promised to meet me again.' Suddenly he was close and she felt his hand under her chin, tilting her face to his. He whispered: 'Oh Vicky, you are an enchantress. You cast spells and no one is safe. Thomas, Edwin Brett—'

'Who takes artistic photographs? Oh Alex, what nonsense!'

'Is it?' She felt his cheek against hers. 'Is it nonsense that I can't stop thinking about you? That I've tried to put you out of my thoughts and haven't succeeded?

Come, don't tantalise me any longer. Who are you, mystery girl? Why are you working as little more than a servant?

'It's all wrong; I won't let you do it. Oh, Vicky, my darling girl!' His mouth found hers and his arms were around her, holding her close against him. She was swept away in a wave of excitement, exaltation and dismay. She had not expected this—or had she? Was this why she had risked discovery and possible dismissal? Had she guessed that to be alone with him in this shadowy little summer-house was dangerous—and thrilling? He was lifting her up, carrying her over to the broad wooden seat, murmuring passionate endearments, kissing her fiercely . . .

'No, *No*! Let me go, Alex, *please*!' She felt his hand on her breast and with sudden strength she tore herself free from his arms, panting and dishevelled. 'You frighten me!'

'Darling girl—' he began, but she had fled, running up the long yew walk, her breath sobbing in her throat. As she drew near the house she paused to gain control. Her hair was in disorder—and where was her cap? Her cheeks burned and her heart still beat like a bird's wing inside her.

She slipped silently up to the nursery, grateful that she met no one on the way. Sue was dozing and thankful to be allowed to go to bed.

Vicky sank into a chair, her thoughts in turmoil. At first, anger blazed against Alex. He had no right to treat her as he had. But slowly her innate honesty told her she had brought it upon herself. To have agreed to meet him at that hour and in so secluded a spot had given him reason to think—what?

'That I'm in love with him and—and—' She sprang up and began to walk up and down the room. How much did she like Alex? Had he truly captured her heart and, if so, what was she going to do about it? His kisses excited her and she had felt an answering passion for a moment. Thinking her alone in the world and forced to earn her living in a menial way, he might consider her fair game for a flirtation. Perhaps he planned to seduce her! He would never consider marrying her unless he knew who she was.

That, of course, was the solution, to tell him she was Sir Andrew Lynton's youngest daughter. Why was she so averse to revealing who she was? Soon she would return to London and would probably meet him on her own ground. Would telling him now spoil her hitherto unacknowledged wish for him to love her honourably as Annie Fisher? What a triumph that would be—and how impossible. Well-born, wealthy young men did not marry nursemaids, and although Alex knew she was not of the servant class, he would not consider she was of his world.

She lay awake a long time that night. Alex was dangerous because he so deeply attracted her and she could not stop herself thinking about him, in spite of his behaviour. A sudden thought startled her.

'If I told him who I was, would he be angry and think I had deliberately fooled him to amuse myself? Would he think I had behaved badly in doing what I've done? Most people would, I suppose.'

She tossed restlessly in her bed until at last sleep came.

To her astonishment, Mr Brett appeared in the nursery shortly after breakfast.

'It is such a fine morning—and the early light is so clear,' he stammered, 'I—I thought I would like to do another study of the children. Perhaps the little girl—Lucy, isn't she?—by the fountain, sitting on the edge and looking down into the water,' he gazed at Vicky with hopeful, shy brown eyes.

'Has Lady Falconer—'

'Oh yes, she will allow it. It will make a charming study. If you could bring her to the Italian garden?'

'Very well, sir. In about half an hour.'

'Thank you so much, Nurse. I shall await you.'

Vicky watched him hurry away, then she turned to Lucy. 'Let's put on one of your pretty dresses, Lucy. Mr Brett wants to take another photograph of you.'

Lucy was pleasantly excited and in a pink velvet dress and fringed sash, with her hair brushed and shining, she accompanied Vicky into the garden where they found Mr Brett fiddling with his camera.

'Ah, there you are! This is splendid.' His eyes lit up as they rested on Vicky and a faint pink suffused his ingenuous face. 'If Lucy will sit on the rim of the fountain, looking down . . .'

The arrangement took some time and Vicky had the impression that Mr Brett was not hurrying himself. His evident interest in her amused her and she answered his questions demurely when he asked where and when she took the children for a walk.

The photograph was taken, and then Mr Brett decided on another pose. Lucy was to stand by a large stone urn, negligently leaning her elbow on it and smiling into the camera. The pose was easy enough, but Lucy's round face failed to register anything more than a sluggish apathy. She had become bored and felt no desire to smile.

'If you could get her to express a little more *vivacity*, Nurse,' Mr Brett urged.

Vicky forebore telling him that vivacity was not one of Lucy's strong points.

'Come, Lucy dear, look a little happier . . .' She broke off as she saw the child's face change.

'Ah, that's better,' Mr Brett exclaimed and dived for his camera. Vicky turned to see what had made Lucy smile so brightly and saw Thomas Craig standing watching them with his usual air of imperturbability.

'Thomas, will you stay and play with me?' Lucy abandoned the urn to run and clutch Thomas's hand. 'Can we play hide and seek? Annie can play too—and Mr Brett.'

'No, Lucy, you must come back to the nursery,' Vicky said hastily without looking at Thomas. 'The dressmaker is coming to measure you for some new dresses, remember?'

Mr Brett emerged from under his black cloth. 'Pray do not leave yet, I would like to show you the studies I took recently.' He picked up a small portfolio and took out some photographs. Vicky went to look at them, accompanied by Lucy, and together they inspected the photographs of the children and the one of Vicky alone with Lucy, and the house-party on the front steps of the house.

'Jolly good, Brett,' Thomas remarked. He took the photographs from Vicky and studied them thoughtfully. 'The children look natural.'

They were interrupted by a group of guests: Miss Effie Grange, Maud, old Lady French, Alex Beaumont and two other men. The photographs were handed around and admired. Effie Grange pronounced the children, 'too deliciously sweet for words', but protested her hair looked quite horrid in the group photograph and smiled up at Alex for the expected denial.

'The nurse comes out the best,' Lady French announced. 'Reminds me of someone who had that same rather mischievous smile . . . Can't remember who at the moment.'

Vicky moved away, grateful for Lady French's uncertain memory. As soon as she could, she grabbed Lucy and retreated towards the house. She had not looked at Alex, but had felt his eyes on her.

'Wait!' It was Thomas's voice and tightening her hand on Lucy's, Vicky increased her pace, pretending not to hear. The last person she wished to see was the perfidious Thomas. But he easily caught up with them.

'Lucy, your mother is in the library, run along and ask her if I can take you for a drive in the park in the dog-cart.'

Lucy rushed off with a squeal of delight and Vicky found herself alone with Thomas, something she wished strongly to avoid. She said quickly,

'I must go and see—'

'You mean you're running away?' She saw the amusement in his eyes and felt her colour rise.

'Rubbish!' It was not, she realised too late, how a nursemaid should talk to one of her employer's guests, but he really was the most infuriating creature! She glared at him. 'Kindly allow me to pass!'

'Not until I have returned this to you.' He pulled something from the pocket of his jacket—her cap. 'It's much better than that appalling thing you've got on your head now.' Before she could move, he had calmly removed the old unbecoming cap, from her head and stood regarding her, his head slightly tilted to one side and his eyes thoughtful. 'You know, I like you better without any cap. Your hair is too attractive to be hidden. You don't have the right type of face to wear a cap.'

She snatched the two caps out of his hands. 'I am not in the least interested in what you think of my hair or my face! And I am not going to stand here listening to you talking nonsense!' She turned sharply, but was halted by his next words.

'You haven't thanked me for being the first person to visit the summer-house this morning and find, and return, your cap.'

A tiny chill crept up her spine as she stared at him.

Had he been in the yew walk last night and, if so, what had he seen and heard?

He shook his head. 'No, I didn't see you last night, but I know you were there and with whom. You are a singularly obstinate and rash young woman, Annie Fisher.'

'And you are a strange friend of Mr Beaumont's,' she flung at him, 'telling lies about him and trying to make people think—'

'Trying to stop a headstrong young woman from imagining herself in love with him.' A sterner note had appeared in his voice and there was no laughter now in his eyes, they were cold and, she thought, a little contemptuous.

Anger made her reckless. 'And suppose I do fall in love with him?'

'Is that quite the way you planned your little escapade to end?'

Shock held her silent. How much did Thomas know about her? He was guessing. He could not know who she really was, but he did know she was no nursemaid.

She turned and walked swiftly away and he made no attempt to follow her.

Lady Falconer nodded when Vicky explained that Lucy was needed in the nursery where Miss Grindly, the dressmaker, awaited her.

'No, Lucy, you cannot drive with Mr Craig this morning. Go with Nurse, like a good little girl.' She turned as her husband entered the room. 'Oh Charles, can you imagine it? Mother insists on coming to us for the ball. *So* ridiculous at her age.'

Vicky took a disappointed Lucy to the nursery where she found a small, bright-eyed woman sitting in the basket chair who rose as they came in.

'Good morning, Nurse. Her ladyship has given me directions about what she wishes. We'll just take measurements now, shall we?'

'Thank you, Miss Grindly. Now stand still, Lucy.'

While she measured Lucy and wrote in her little notebook, Miss Grindly chatted.

'Grown quite a bit, hasn't she? My, but I'm pleased you're here, Nurse Annie, and not that Brodmin creature. Proper difficult she was, and never a friendly word for anyone. She told me I didn't stroke my pleats, now can you believe it?'

Vicky said no, she could not believe it, and wondered how one stroked one's pleats. Sue came in with a tray of tea and everyone settled down for a gossip.

'So there's to be a grand ball,' Miss Grindly remarked, sipping her tea in a refined manner. 'My, there'll be some elegant Paris fashions, I'll be bound. Society ladies and their handsome gentlemen. Maybe you'll get a chance to see something of it. When I was doing the household sewing at Greystone Manor a ball was held and some of us watched from the garden. A regular treat it was, all those fine gowns and the *jewels*—well you wouldn't believe!'

'Don't seem right to me that some people have all that jewellery when pore folk sometimes hasn't enough to eat,' Sue said austerely.

'Well, as it happened, there was something very dreadful . . .' She stopped as James the footman put his head around the door.

'Mr Brett would like to have a word with Nurse Fisher in the morning room right away.' He winked at Vicky. 'Now you take care, Nurse. You can't always trust these artistic gents.'

'James!' Sue chided indignantly as Vicky rose, wondering why on earth Mr Brett should wish to speak to her.

He came to meet her as she entered the room.

'Oh Nurse, I am sorry to trouble you. I trust I haven't interrupted your duties?'

'No, sir. You wanted to speak to me?'

'Well, yes, I do. You may remember my showing the photographic studies I had made to some people in the Italian garden this morning . . .'

'Oh yes, I do.'

'Well, I've wondered if Lucy . . . or if you noticed anyone . . . You see, that study of the little girl and you has vanished.'

'Vanished?'

'Yes indeed. When I took the photographs back to my room I found there was one missing.' He blushed as he met her eyes. 'It was—was a study I especially—er—considered one of my best efforts and I cannot imagine how I could have lost it—or who would have taken it. Do you have any suggestions, Nurse?'

'I'm afraid not, Mr Brett. Lucy certainly did not take it and nor did I.'

'Oh I didn't mean for a moment that I thought you . . . Perhaps one of the ladies took it by mistake.'

'Have you asked them?'

'Well, yes, I have, and no one seems to know anything. I have made a thorough search of my room. I just wanted to ask you if you had *any* idea of how I might have lost it.'

'You know, I don't believe you have lost it,' Vicky told him. 'Someone has taken it by mistake and forgotten about it. I'm sure it will turn up soon.'

'I trust so. I am very grateful to you. I—I hope I have not been a nuisance.' He gazed at her with hopeful brown eyes that reminded her of a pet spaniel she had once owned. 'Do you . . . will you be taking the children for a walk in the park this afternoon?'

Vicky told him it depended on the weather and if the children were to have riding lessons, and escaped before he could ask further questions.

How lucky he had not thought of asking her if one of

the *gentlemen* might have purloined her photograph. She had not seen Alex pocket it, but she guessed he had it, and he had taken it because he had fallen in love with her! There could be no other reason.

CHAPTER
NINE

EXCITEMENT was mounting in Wellbury Court and it seemed to Vicky that the house hummed with activity like an alerted beehive.

More guests had arrived, among them old Mrs Dreyer who wept over the children at their first meeting which was in the park when she saw Vicky and her grand-children walking and made the groom stop her carriage. Thomas was with her.

'Such lovely little darlings,' Mrs Dreyer sighed, mopping her eyes, 'and so well-behaved.'

'Don't you believe it,' Thomas said. 'The boys can fight like little demons, and Lucy howls if she isn't allowed a second piece of cake.'

'Thomas! I cannot believe that.'

'Ask their nurse. Luckily she knows how to deal with these tantrums.'

Vicky looked away, determined to ignore him.

'Are you going to dance at the ball, Grandmama?' Giles asked with interest.

'Dear me, no, darling. Grandmama is too old to dance, you know. I shall sit and watch the pretty ladies in their lovely gowns.'

'Will they wear beautiful jewels?' Lucy asked.

'Oh yes, I expect so.' Mrs Dreyer turned to Thomas. 'I suppose Lady Grange will have the famous emerald necklace with her. They are really more suitable for her age, I always think she should let dear Effie have her pearls, pearls look best on a young girl.'

'Better than emeralds? Possibly—unless the girl has silver-green eyes.'

Vicky grabbed Lucy's hand. 'I am afraid we must return for tea, Mrs Dreyer.'

'Can Thomas come to tea with us today?' Mark asked. The two other children added their pleas and, to Vicky's annoyance, Thomas announced that he would meet them in the nursery in a quarter of an hour, a proceeding that met with Mrs Dreyer's approval.

'I have always thought it a pity their mother keeps the children so isolated from the rest of the household. Now, when you were young, Thomas, I remember you had your meals with your family and your dear mother often took you with her when she went visiting.'

'Where I was very definitely unwanted and made a complete nuisance of myself,' Thomas remarked.

'Why? What did you do?' the boys demanded in one voice.

'I dare not tell you, your nurse would be shocked.'

'Oh no she wouldn't. Tell us!'

'I upset the cream jug over my hostess's dress, trod on the cat's tail and put a cream éclair on the Vicar's chair.'

'Did he sit on it?'

'Yes.'

'Was he *very* angry?'

'He restrained himself to a few rather bitter remarks about original sin,' Thomas told them. 'Now run back and see if you can persuade the housekeeper to give you some gingersnaps, they're my favourites.'

'You said chocolate biscuits were your favourites,' Lucy said.

'They come pretty close. Ask for some chocolate biscuits too and let's be thoroughly greedy.'

The children giggled in delight. As they walked away, Vicky asked Giles,

'Why do you like Mr Craig so much?'

He considered. 'I don't know, Mark and me just do.'

As she spread the tea-cloth over the green chenille tablecloth on the nursery table, Vicky wondered if Thomas would take this opportunity to repeat his warning about Alex. She prepared to treat any such attempt with icy disdain.

However when he had been greeted enthusiastically by the children, he proceeded to engage them and Sue in conversation while consuming quantities of gingersnaps and chocolate biscuits, and paid Vicky small attention. Most irrationally she found herself resenting this almost as much as if he had started scolding her. That someone of so little account in her life, so unworthy of her notice, should by his lack of attention arouse in her a desire to have a row with him was humiliating. Yes she knew she was wishing she could break through his unruffled calm. If only she could tell him what she thought of him and his behaviour towards Alex . . . But of course it was impossible, much as she would like to fling her dislike and contempt in his face.

She was not aware her feelings could be read so easily until he turned to her and said,

'Perhaps it was a mistake to ask for gingersnaps, ginger *can* inflame the emotions—in some people, you know, it acts as an irritant.'

She pretended not to hear and continued to spread jam on Lucy's slice of bread and butter. She would *not* let him make her lose her temper!

Suddenly she heard Mark say: 'Mr Brett told us he has lost one of his photographs, the one of Annie and Lucy. He lost it the day he showed it to all those people. Do you think one of them stole it?'

'I expect so,' his twin said sagely. 'Some person liked the picture so much they stole it, like a burglar. P'raps they wanted to look at Annie.'

Mark nodded agreement. 'No one would want to look at *Lucy*.'

To her great annoyance, Vicky felt the colour creep into her face under Thomas's speculative gaze. Had he guessed who the thief was? Not that it mattered if he had; it had nothing to do with him.

It was only when he had gone, taking the children with him to pay a visit to the new kittens, that she realised how much of her thoughts he had occupied during tea and how conscious she had been of his presence and how little he had been of hers. The knowledge piqued her, and she was glad when the next visitor to the nursery proved to be her sister Maud.

'Mama has written,' Maud said, sinking into a chair. 'She has not enjoyed Montana very much, I'm afraid. The climate has not suited her and she does not seem to have taken the right clothes for it. She is looking forward to visiting Wilbur's family in Boston and plans to stay there for a little to see something of American society. Vicky, you *will* stop being a nurse soon, won't you? I mean, if Father and Mama find out . . . *I* shan't say anything of course, but—'

'I know you won't, dear Maud, I have complete faith in your discretion,' Vicky assured her. 'Now, tell me what is happening downstairs. We are insulated from all news up here. Are you busy preparing for the ball? Will you be wearing your white lace dress?'

'Yes, and the pink gauze scarf and the ostrich fan Mama has lent me. Effie Grange is to wear pale blue moiré with rosebud trimming, and her mother has a new Paris model, but Effie says the colour doesn't really suit her, it's rather a vivid saffron.'

'Not too good with the famous emeralds, I should think.'

'Well, she did intend to wear them, but Effie has persuaded her to wear the pearls instead.' Maud leaned back in her chair, smiling dreamily. 'Archie says I shall have his mother's pearls when we are married.'

'I consider you deserve them, Maud dear. Now tell me, is Effie still forbidden to approach Alex Beaumont?'

'Oh well, of course she cannot *ignore* him, it would cause comment, wouldn't it? But Lady Grange isn't being very kind and poor Effie has to pretend she does not care for him and of course she *does*. And he does continue to pay her quite marked attention, in spite of her mother's disapproval. I sometimes think he does it solely to tease Lady Grange.'

Vicky had the same thought. Alex would be ironically amused at the old lady's obvious attempts to keep him and Effie apart and would probably find a wicked enjoyment in pretending a passion for her daughter.

Vicky had enlisted Mrs Dreyer's help in persuading Lady Falconer to agree to the children being allowed to stay up late to see the beginning of the ball. One of the long french windows would be uncurtained so it could be opened if the heat became excessive and the children— well wrapped up—could watch from the terrace outside.

More guests arrived, and at last the great day came. As the hours advanced the life of the great house quickened with sounds of hurried footsteps, doors opening and shutting and calls for maids. An occasional whiff of scorching hair came from those rooms where fringes were being curled, and Miss Grindly, the dressmaker, was much in demand to adjust the fit of a bodice, make a rearrangement of a skirt drapery and stitch up something that had 'gone at the gathers'. Sue made frequent excursions to the kitchen quarters and came back with accounts of minor disasters, a burned sauce, one of the cats having got at the fish, and the behaviour of some of the visiting lady's-maids.

'Threw her hairbrush at her maid, one lady did, and cut her cheek. Lady Grange's girl said there'd been a scene with Miss Grange whose eyes had gone pink and she's had to ask the still-room maid for witch-hazel to bathe them. I had a peep into the dining-room and it looks just lovely with carnations and smilax and serviettes done up to look like water-lilies . . .' Sue paused for breath.

The children became excited and impatient. At last the time came for them to be swathed in coats and shawls and taken down through the house and out onto the long stone terrace outside the ballroom windows. The blaze of light made them blink as they stared through the window at the couples whirling gracefully past in a waltz. Music from the orchestra reached them and memories of dancing to the entrancing strains of Waldteufel's Skaters' Waltz made Vicky's toes tingle and her eyes glow.

She saw Lady Falconer, slim and graceful in pale green chiffon, a delicate diamond tiara on her elaborate coiffure, languidly waving her fan while she talked to a stout, bearded man Vicky recognised as head of a noble house and a friend of her father. Rose-shaded lights gleamed on silks and satins, on spangled net and silver tissue, on tiaras, dog-collars of diamonds, bracelets and rings, on emeralds, rubies, garnets and amethysts. A distinguished foreigner wore a scarlet ribbon across his chest. Mr Brett's coat-tails whirled as he spun his partner. Mrs Dreyer, slightly moist of eye and wearing plum satin, sat with the other dowagers amongst whom Vicky saw Lady Grange in her saffron gown, with her pearls displayed on her ample bosom. So Effie's advice had been taken.

'I think Mama looks the prettiest,' Lucy declared.

'There's Thomas talking to old Lady French,' Giles exclaimed. 'Can I call to him?'

'Certainly not, and anyway he wouldn't hear you,' Vicky said. She was watching the brilliant throng of dancers in search of Alex, but had not discovered him yet. Perhaps he had slipped away with Effie . . . No, Effie, demure in pale blue taffeta, was dancing with a slim, languid young man who managed to look as bored as she did.

Suddenly she saw Alex and caught her breath. How handsome he looked in evening dress and how easy and debonair his manner! He was watching the dancers, a touch of mockery in his smile as he listened to what a woman beside him was saying.

The waltz ended and the dancers began to drift out of the room. Vicky saw Maud surrounded by an admiring little group of men paying homage to 'one of the beautiful Miss Lyntons' and hoped her sister was not missing the faithful Archie too greatly.

'The wind's getting up,' Sue whispered in Vicky's ear, 'we'd best be getting back to the nursery.'

Vicky agreed reluctantly and they retreated up to the nursery rooms to put the sleepy children to bed and sit down to supper. After they had eaten, Sue slipped away, no doubt to seek word with James who, resplendent in scarlet coat and white breeches, had been in attendance on the guests at supper.

Vicky picked up some sewing, then threw it aside. The scene in the ballroom had stirred her blood and the lilt of the music was still in her ears. She began to pace the room restlessly. Suddenly she swung around and caught up Sue's dark cloak; she must look at the ballroom scene once more!

Music throbbed through the house and the scent of hot-house flowers was everywhere. The kitchen staff were enjoying a late supper and no one saw her as she slipped out of a back door and into the velvet darkness of the night.

She ran swiftly around the side of the house. Suddenly she paused, startled by a sound that seemed to come

from somewhere above her. She was standing under-
neath the balcony which Alex had once condemned as
being unsafe. It came again, a scraping, slithering sound.
There was no moon and the starlight did little to dispel
the darkness. Instinctively she shrank back into the
shadow of the archway that led into the yew walk. The
sound grew louder and now she thought she could see
something moving, dark against darkness. Someone was
coming down one of the verandah supports which had a
thick vine twined around it.

Her mouth felt dry and a chill of fear crept over her as
she strained her eyes to make out the figure. It was a man
in evening dress, the patch of white that was a shirt
showing dimly as he reached the ground and turned. He
paused, and the next minute she heard him curse softly
and saw the sudden glow of a torch as he bent to search
the ground, evidently for something he had dropped.
Then the torch was switched off and he had gone, his feet
making no sound on the dewy lawn.

Vicky stood still, clutching Sue's cloak around her,
astonishment and shock making her mind whirl. For a
brief second the light of the torch had caught the man's
face. What was Thomas Craig doing climbing down from
the balcony while the rest of the guests were dancing?

She did not know how long she stood in the shadow of
the archway. Thomas *could* have been playing some
trick. She knew four bedrooms opened onto the balcony. But why should he wish to take a risk of being
found out or falling? The bedrooms would all be empty
as the maids were downstairs at supper. Thomas's bedroom, she knew, was on the other side of the house.

Had he taken a dare to climb the balcony in the dark?
But surely if someone had bet him he could not do it he
would have been there to see Thomas succeed.

While she puzzled over it, a small, insistent thought
that had been hovering at the back of her mind came to

the fore; Thomas was not a man to accept such a senseless, positively childish dare. She could almost hear him say, with raised eyebrows and a derisive grin: 'Climb up there in my evening clothes? Not a chance, old fellow!'

Yet he *had* done exactly that.

She became aware she was shivering. All desire to watch the dancing left her and she turned and went back slowly to the nursery. Would she tell Thomas she had seen him? Would she tell anyone? Was it possible that Thomas, so extremely unromantic, was having an affair with someone and had taken on the highly unsuitable role of Romeo? She almost laughed as she thought of it. Who would be his Juliet, one of the pert lady's-maids?

Sue had not returned. Vicky looked at the sleeping children, tucked a blanket more securely around Lucy, and went to her room. She lay awake for some time, listening to the distant music and puzzling over Thomas's odd behaviour. It all seemed so unlike him; but perhaps she did not know him so well after all.

Her first thought next morning was that she must have slept late. Sounds came from the floors below and she could hear voices raised in excitement. She sprang out of bed and found it was her usual hour of waking and wondered at the bustle that appeared to be taking place. After last night she had expected everyone to sleep late and the servants to do their work as silently as possible.

She dressed slowly, still half-awake, and decided to let the children sleep on after the night's excitement.

When she went into the nursery there was no sign of Sue and no sign of breakfast. Evidently the festivities had thrown the smooth working of the household somewhat out of order. She was halfway down the back stairs when she met Sue.

'Sue, what is happening? Where is breakfast? I am longing for my tea.'

'Oh, Nurse Annie! Such a dreadful thing! We might all have been murdered in our beds!' Sue's eyes were popping with excitement and her thin bosom heaved dramatically.

'What on earth are you talking about?' Vicky demanded. '*What* dreadful thing?'

'Why, Lady Grange's famous emeralds have gone—stolen right away! There's ever such a to-do. The police have come and there's questions being asked, and Lady Grange's maid is in hysterics and no good to anyone, the silly piece!'

'The emeralds stolen? From her room, you mean? Of course, she didn't wear them last night, did she? Who could have taken them?'

'I expect the police'll find out, they're to search the whole house, James says, and he says they'll search all of us too!' She shuddered in delighted horror.

Vicky waited until she had her voice under control, then she said,

'Well, that's no reason for us to miss breakfast. Go and get it, please, Sue.'

She watched the girl hurry down the stairs. A slow chill was invading her and she shivered as she recalled Alex's words when he had spoken of Thomas: 'Thomas is clever . . . he defended a receiver of stolen goods . . . the man was obviously guilty . . . he seems to get to all the big house-parties . . .'

It could not be true! Thomas Craig, sneak-thief who haunted wealthy mansions where society women were careless about their jewels. It simply was not possible. He was a successful barrister and had no need to turn to crime—or had he? Was there a vicious streak hidden in him somewhere? He had once been poor and had perhaps suffered hardship which brought a resentment of the careless, wealthy world he now lived in, a resentment that had festered until he saw no crime in stealing from it. She remembered Maud had said something about a robbery in Scotland; had Thomas been there?

'I suppose I ought to tell someone about last night,' she thought uneasily.

Whom should she tell? Alex? The police? Sir Charles? The sight of Sue returning with breakfast made her realise how long she had been standing on the stairs while her mind ran in dizzying circles.

Sue managed to restrain her excitement and no mention of the robbery was made before the children. The boys went to the schoolroom and Lucy to her riding lesson. An air of suppressed excitement was everywhere. Most of the guests were still in their rooms while the police established themselves in the library for the questioning of the household.

Vicky wondered if she would be summoned. No one knew of her presence near the balcony last night and her uneasiness increased as she realised Lady Falconer would certainly be extremely angry to know the children had been left alone while their nurse amused herself wandering in the garden. She might be dismissed and that would be decidedly awkward since her parents were not due to return to England just yet. It would be unwise to return to London where someone might recognise her and report to Lady Lynton. Maud would be no help, and anyway it would be unfair to involve her in further deception.

She was still feeling confused and uncertain when she and Sue were sent for, but as the first questions were asked, the confusion fell away and she heard herself answering calmly and confidently, almost as if she were being automatically prompted.

No, she had not left the nursery after taking the children back from the terrace. No, she had not seen or heard anything unusual or noticed any strangers about.

She had slept soundly and knew nothing of the robbery until Sue had told her.

Sue, pale with excitement, admitted visiting the kitchens 'to get a cup of hot milk' and wisely did not mention the length of her visit. She was agog to discuss the burglary, but Vicky felt she must be alone to pull her thoughts into some sort of order and leaving Lucy in Sue's care, she shut herself in her bedroom.

She was guilty of concealing important evidence and she was not sure what the verdict would be if she were found out. Why had she done it? If Thomas was innocent and there was some harmless explanation of what he had done, it would not matter if she spoke out. If he *was* guilty, then she was guilty too in hiding from the police what she knew. Too late she wished she had not let some obscure instinct lead her into telling lies.

'I should have told them and let them find out if he is the man they are seeking,' she thought unhappily. 'I've made a wretched mess of things! If only I could talk to someone.'

CHAPTER
TEN

MRS DREYER sent a message to say she wanted to take the three children out for a drive in the park before lunch. When she had dressed the children and delivered them to their grandmother, Vicky went back to the nursery to find Maud awaiting her.

'Oh, Vicky, isn't it simply *terrible*? Poor Lady Grange is in such a state of shock that the doctor had to be sent for. The police are all over the place asking questions and Effie's maid says they suspect *her* and she won't stay another minute if her character is going to be taken away. Just imagine, while we were all dancing downstairs and enjoying ourselves, a burglar was creeping about the house looking for something to steal!' Maud's huge blue eyes were wide with horror.

'I think he knew exactly what it was he wanted to steal,' Vicky said, collapsing on to the window seat. She felt extraordinarily tired and her head was beginning to ache. 'Those emeralds are famous. What a pity Lady Grange did not wear them last night.'

'That is what she keeps telling poor Effie, she blames *her* because she said the necklace didn't go well with the dress. Effie can't stop crying, she says how could she know a burglar was waiting to steal them.'

'Well, how could she? Have the police any idea how the burglary was done?'

'I heard Sir Charles say something about the balcony,' Vicky felt her heart give a jerk, 'they seem to think someone *could* have climbed up it. Lady Grange's bedroom opens onto it, you know. It wouldn't be very difficult to climb, Mr Brett said—we were looking at it this morning—because of the vine growing up one of the pillars.'

With an effort, Vicky kept her voice casual: 'Were there any foot-prints or anything?'

'I don't think they found any, it rained early this morning, you know, and the gardener had taken the wheelbarrow over the ground.'

'It would have been dangerous to climb the balcony at night, it was very dark.'

'Well, I suppose the thief thought it worth the risk. Someone said the police think it *might* be someone in the house, but Mr Brett says it is not likely as the staff have been here for years and what could they do with a famous emerald necklace? He wanted to take a photograph of a policeman standing under the balcony, but they wouldn't let him.' She looked at her sister and giggled. 'Do you know, I think Mr Brett is quite taken with you. He has asked me several times about you and I have been frightened I might let out something.'

'Then please be careful. Does Lady Grange remain here?'

'No, she and Effie want to leave as soon as they can—at least, Effie doesn't really want to leave because Alex Beaumont is staying on. She says he has been so kind and understanding over this horrid business. I think her mother is being very unfair because it was—' she stopped as Sue came in to say Miss Grindly wished to know when it would be convenient to try on Lucy's new dresses.

'Oh, this afternoon, I suppose.' Vicky rose. 'Thank you for coming to ask about the children, Miss Lynton, we've kept the news of the burglary from them up to now.'

Maud rose hurriedly. 'Yes—er—Nurse Annie. I expect they would get excited, children do, don't they? I must go.' She retreated and Sue said admiringly,

'Lovely, isn't she? A real beauty, not like Miss Grange as is only pretty, to my mind.'

The children returned, bubbling with excitement, their grandmother having told them of the burglary and the wicked man who had crept into the house while the ball was in progress and stolen a beautiful necklace of green stones.

'She wept when she told us,' Giles said. '*I* don't think it's sad. I'm going to look for the burglar, Mark and me think he's hiding in the garden somewhere. Will the police give us a reward if we find him, Annie?'

'Perhaps—I don't know. Wash your hands for lunch, children. Lucy, the dressmaker will be here this afternoon to try on your new dresses.'

Lady Falconer paid an unexpected visit to the nursery soon after lunch. She looked a little pale and her manner was nervous and irritable.

'It is really *too* annoying that their grandmother had to tell the children . . . Now they will think of nothing else. No, Giles and Mark, I will *not* answer silly questions, I want you to forget about it. Really, at a time like this . . . Mr Beaumont has kindly offered to take the children out for a drive in his motor and give them tea somewhere. It will take their minds off this dreadful business.'

'Miss Grindly wants to try on Lucy's dresses—' Vicky began just as the door opened and the dressmaker came in.

'Oh Miss Grindly,' Lady Falconer said impatiently, 'be quick, the children are going out.'

'I want Annie to come with us,' Lucy announced.

'Don't be silly, Lucy, Annie has work to do here.'

'I want Annie to come,' Lucy repeated stubbornly.

'Now don't be naughty, Lucy.'

'I'll wriggle and wriggle and Miss Grindly won't be

able to make my dresses,' Lucy said with unusual determination.

'She'll make us late,' Mark wailed. 'Oh, let Annie come if she wants it, *we* don't mind.'

Lady Falconer put a hand to her head, looking distracted. 'Children, you are making my head ache! For heaven's sake, Nurse, go with them. Don't let Lucy eat too many sweet cakes, and don't let them talk about this wretched burglary. It's really *too* dreadful to think such a thing should have happened here!'

Miss Grindly's pinnings and shortenings and re-fittings were soon over and the children ready.

Alex's Delage was in the front drive with Alex at the wheel. When he saw Vicky he pulled off his motor goggles and leaned forward, saying under his breath,

'You're coming with us? That's ripping! I've been trying to see you, but with all this trouble—'

'Can I sit beside you?' Giles interrupted.

'*I* made Mama let Annie come with us,' Lucy said complacently.

'Then you are most certainly assured of a place in heaven,' Alex said, his eyes on Vicky's charmingly flushed face and sparkling eyes. 'Into the car, all of you.'

Vicky's spirits rose as they left Wellbury Court. The country had the muted beauty of late autumn. Lines of bare trees spread in a lacy pattern against the pale sky and the red-brown of ploughed fields and green pastureland were veiled in soft lavender haze. On either side the land rose in gentle hills patched with fields and fell into dreaming valleys cradling thatched cottages clustering around grey square-towered churches.

It was delightful to get away from the nursery and her duties there and be with Alex who had once called her 'my darling girl' and who, she guessed, would somehow manage to get her alone.

She considered whether she should tell him about

what she had seen last night. Would he leap to the conclusion that Thomas was the thief and would he go to the police?

For some reason she found herself unwilling to speak out, at least not yet. Perhaps the police were already on the track of the thief and to say anything about what she had seen would be wasting their time for which they would certainly not be grateful.

She was brought out of her musings by hearing Alex say,

'We'll stop for tea in the next town, there's quite a decent little hotel.'

'Do we have to eat bread and butter?' Mark asked anxiously.

'Not unless you crave it,' Alex told him. 'There are some pet rabbits in the garden, you may be allowed to play with them. Will that be in order, Nurse?'

'I'm sure the children will enjoy that,' she said demurely.

Tea—without bread and butter—was a success and Vicky looked the other way when Lucy took her fourth cake. The boot-boy volunteered to show the children the rabbits. When they had gone, Alex leaned forward eagerly.

'You've been cruel, Vicky, hiding yourself from me. You must know how much I want to see you.'

'There was all this upset about the burglary . . . Alex, do you think someone broke into the house? Most of the doors were locked and there were no windows smashed.'

He shrugged. 'Someone must have got in somehow.'

'Could the thief have been let in by an accomplice?'

His brows rose. 'I suppose you mean one of the staff? You surely can't suspect one of the guests.'

'No, only . . . *Do* you think the police suspect something like that?'

'If they do, they aren't saying anything about it. They

have questioned everyone and searched the house and no doubt the county police are alerted.'

'I hope they find the thief soon,' she said restlessly. 'It's horrible suspecting someone—' she broke off abruptly. Alex was staring at her.

'Do *you* suspect someone, Vicky?'

'No—no, of course not,' she said hastily. 'I—I meant that it isn't pleasant to think someone was prowling around the house last night.'

His eyes had grown uncomfortably intent. 'I think you meant more than that. You aren't adept at hiding anything, Vicky, your charming face gives you away. Did you see or hear anything last night?'

She avoided his eyes. 'How could I, I was in the nursery except for the time when Sue and I took the children to the terrace to watch the dancing.' She decided to change the subject and said lightly: 'Wasn't it a splendid sight? All those pretty women and their lovely gowns and the flowers and music. I could hear the music when I went back to the nursery and it was so enticing I simply *had* to take another look—' She stopped, and knew it was too late by the sudden flash of interest in his eyes.

'—take another look at the ball?' he asked softly. 'That was not what you told the police.'

She looked down at the table. 'I—I must have forgotten. They bothered me with so many questions. Anyway, it was not important.'

'Of course not—unless you saw or heard something that might have interested them.' Suddenly his voice was hard. '*Did* you see anything? I think you had better tell me, Vicky.'

'But it probably wasn't important—and I would rather not say any more.'

There was a silence in which she could feel her nerves slowly tightening.

Alex said quietly: 'If you can't confide in me, I shall be forced to tell the police you know something and they will question you and it could be a little . . . unpleasant for you.'

She put her hand to her head which had begun to throb, her mind confused. What obscure urge had made her keep silent about Thomas? If he was guilty, he must be caught and the emeralds recovered. If he was innocent, he was safe. She could trust Alex; he might not like Thomas, but he would be fair in his judgment—and she *must* tell someone!

'I did go outside a second time. Someone came down from the balcony on the west side. I hid in the shadow of the archway.'

'Did you see who it was?' Alex asked sharply.

'It was very dark, you know.'

'Was it one of the servants?'

'I—I think he was in evening dress, I thought I saw his white shirt front.'

'Then it was not quite so dark. What did he do?'

'He slid down the pillar that has the vine growing on it, and seemed to search for something he had dropped. He had a torch.'

'Then you must have seen him. Your face has given you away; you know who it was—and you are going to tell me. My dearest girl, surely you know you can trust me?'

'But you don't really like or trust him,' she stammered unhappily, 'and you may be prejudiced—'

'*Thomas!*' She winced at the sudden grip of his hand on hers. 'My God! It was he you saw last night! Why did you not say something of this?'

'But Alex, it doesn't exactly *prove* he stole anything . . . There could be some explanation . . .' her voice faltered as she realised how weak the words sounded.

Alex sprang up and began to pace the room, his head

bent and his brows drawn over stern eyes.

'I sincerely hope there *is* an explanation, but . . . I've always been puzzled about Thomas. He's never short of money, he does himself very well for a man of the law. But I never for a moment suspected . . .' He swung around on her, his handsome face grim. 'The theft of those pearls at the McDonaldsons' place in Scotland—Thomas was there I remember.'

'You think he stole them?' Vicky caught her breath, then said slowly: 'I will have to tell the authorities.'

He thrust his hands deep into the pockets of his norfolk jacket and stood staring out of the window, frowning.

'What made you keep silent about this?'

'I suppose I couldn't really believe he would do such a thing.' She rose, sighing. 'I'll tell the police. Lady Falconer will dismiss me when she knows I left the children alone for a time last night. Sue wasn't there, you see.'

'No,' he came to her and put his hands on her shoulders. 'I'm not dragging you into this. We're leaving the police out of it. I'm tackling Thomas. He hasn't left the house and he won't dare to go off too soon, it would look suspicious. He'll give me the emeralds—or face a prison sentence.'

'But ought not the police to know—'

'The necklace will be discovered in some place overlooked in the search, I will see to that. And I will make it plain to Thomas I will speak out if anything like this ever occurs again.'

'I suppose *we* are breaking the law, that is, if he *is* the thief.'

'Do you still doubt him? I'm not risking prosecution for withholding information for *his* sake. His mother is delicate, an invalid, and she worships him. The shock would kill her.'

'Oh then we must do as you say,' Vicky said impulsively. 'It is generous of you, Alex, to give him this chance.'

'I've known him and his family all my life, his father was a fine man. I do not wish his memory smirched, Vicky.'

The children came running in, full of how they had played with the rabbits and a puppy. As they all went out to the motor, Alex whispered,

'Meet me tonight.'

She shook her head. 'Not tonight; another time.'

'But I must see you, Vicky, my sweetest girl. I am going to get you out of that wretched nursery, you have no right to be there! I have plans—'

'Giles sat in the front coming so I'm sitting in front on the way back,' Mark broke in.

'Oh all right. Climb in—and don't fiddle with anything.'

Vicky was aware of little but her own thoughts on the drive back. She had wanted to escape the boredom of her life as a débutante, and coming to Wellbury Court as Annie Fisher had seemed an amusing escapade tinged with romance. She had not foreseen complications. Alex was a complication. *Was* she falling in love with him? He had the power, certainly, to stir her emotions.

'But why should that make me uneasy?' she thought. 'If he had no interest in me . . . but he has. He's in love with me, or very nearly. Isn't that what I want? Something like that must have been at the back of my mind when I took Lizzie's place at Wellbury Court. His "plans" for me must mean marriage!'

She glanced at him, at his handsome profile as he turned to answer some question of Mark's, the wide shoulders and faintly arrogant set of his head that distinguished him from other men. He had shown an unexpected generosity towards Thomas. 'If Thomas *is* guilty.' Why should the thought slip into her mind when

Alex, who knew so much more than she did, was convinced of Thomas's guilt?

She sighed, her mind weary of uncertainties and questions without answers, and the nursery, isolated from so many of the frets of the rest of the house, suddenly seemed a haven of peace and security. Once there, she could shut the door on enquiring police officers, restless staff and shocked and troubled visitors.

Next morning her first thought was of Alex and what he would say to Thomas, and if he had recovered the emeralds and how he planned for them to be 'found' somewhere in the house. Alex would find a way to let her know. Perhaps he would meet her when she took the children in the park, although the weather was not encouraging.

The weather did not improve. Heavy slate-coloured clouds moved menacingly across an indigo sky and there was a smell of rain. But Vicky was determined to get out of the house. She wanted to walk swiftly, the wind in her face, and to feel her body tingle with the wintry bite in the air. Lucy, however, was showing signs of a cold and Sir Charles had taken the boys out riding.

'You go out for a turn in the park,' Sue urged, 'you're looking peaky, and no wonder with all that's been happening. I'll keep Miss Lucy warm and give her cinnamon and milk and a lozenge if her throat's rough.'

Gladly Vicky escaped. Once she was free of the gardens, the wind caught her, whipping her coat around her and teasing her dark curls from under her bonnet. She laughed aloud and quickened her pace, delighting in the boisterous weather. She came to a long wall that enclosed the park and found a gate onto a narrow lane that went in the direction of the village.

So far she had not walked outside the estate; now, she determined to follow the lane until she came to another gate. A few drops of rain did not deter her. The swift wind seemed to blow away uneasy thoughts and speculations.

The lane was narrow, its surface churned by the feet of cattle. A high bank topped with a thick hedge rose on one side and the six-foot brick wall on the other. As she came out of the gate she saw ahead of her a man in a waterproof cape and tweed cap. He turned and she saw it was Thomas.

He waited for her. Her first instinct was to retreat hurriedly, but a flash of stubborn pride made her walk forward, her chin raised and her eyes cold.

'You've chosen a bad day for a walk,' were his first words, 'it's going to rain any minute.'

'I don't mind. I felt I wanted a walk.'

'And what you want to do, you do, even if it is sometimes unwise.' He fell into step beside her, apparently unaware of or undisturbed by her chilly air. 'That could get you into trouble, Nurse Annie Fisher.'

'If you are going to start warning me again—' she began hotly, but he interrupted her by saying mildly: 'Oh no, you are far too obstinate to take any sensible advice.'

'I do not consider your advice to be in any way sensible.'

'But you will—and it may be too late. You are a singularly self-willed and headstrong young woman, and surprisingly unlike your sisters.'

Shock held her silent for a moment. 'What—what do you mean?' she stammered at last.

He eyed her thoughtfully. 'Perhaps it is being the last Miss Lynton. With all those doe-eyed little beauties before you, you felt you must be different from them. But you know, you really don't have to try, you *are* different. For one thing, your eyes are silver-green—and more green than silver at the moment.'

She was shaken. How had he found her out? Did he mean to give her away?

'How did you know?' she demanded.

'I saw you at the Devonshire House ball when you stood near. I was talking to Alex and you were staring at him. Your father was beckoning to you; I know Sir Andrew by sight.'

'On the train . . .'

'No, that appalling hat fooled me. But once I got a good look at you I recognised the last Miss Lynton playing at being a nurse.'

She found nothing at all to say to this. They walked in silence for some time, Thomas apparently perfectly at ease and she in a ferment of angry apprehension.

Suddenly Thomas stood still, staring ahead. 'What's that noise?'

For the first time Vicky became aware of an odd mixture of sounds somewhere ahead of them. Men shouting, and a sullen, harsh bellowing that sent a prickle of fear through her. The lane took a bend and there was nothing to be seen, but the medley of sounds was coming nearer.

Suddenly terror rose in icy waves over her! Around the bend came a great bull, his horns tossing as he bellowed defiance at the shouting men pursuing him! She was paralysed with fear as she saw the wicked head with its fiery eyes jerk up as the beast caught sight of them. The thunder of its hoofs and the menacing roar seemed to fill the narrow lane as it bore down on them!

Then she saw Thomas run forward and heard herself scream: 'No! Come back! He'll kill you!'

He paid no attention to her. As the great beast came near, it slackened its approach, its evil eyes fastened upon Thomas, one hoof pawing the ground.

It happened so swiftly she was bewildered. With a

quick movement, Thomas flung the cape he had worn at the bull where it caught on its horns. The next moment Vicky felt herself being grabbed and hoisted up the wall!

'Catch the top and pull yourself up,' Thomas snapped, giving her a final and undignified boost. She managed to grab the top of the wall and haul herself over it and tumble down on the other side where luckily some bushes broke her fall. She lay there dazed, hearing shouts and yells and bellows in the lane.

'Get that rope over him while's he's blind!'

'Bill's got the second rope . . .'

'Stand back . . . get him through that gate, blast the brute!'

She looked up to see Thomas standing over her. He held out his hands and she let him pull her to her feet. Her bonnet had fallen off and her dark curls hung in disorder to her shoulders. She was still trembling and her face was white. Her gloves had torn on the rough bricks and one hand was grazed and bleeding. She stood passively, too shaken by her recent danger to speak while he took out a handkerchief and bound her injured hand.

He said: 'Sit on that tree stump and get your breath back. It was rather a nasty few minutes, wasn't it? What the devil the farmer meant by letting a dangerous beast like that escape . . . But they seem to have got control of him. It was a lucky thing I had that cape with me. It won't be much use now, I'll have to borrow one until I go to London.'

He was talking to give her time to recover. His eyes were on her face and he said abruptly,

'Good, you've got some colour in your face. You've had a bad shock, but you didn't panic or faint.'

She managed a wavering smile. 'It wouldn't have done much good if I had, would it? If you hadn't been so quick—and so brave . . .'

'The instinct of self-preservation is extraordinarily

strong in the human race. Do you feel well enough to walk back to the house?'

She rose. 'Yes. I'm just feeling a little limp. You see, I don't often face a mad bull or scramble up a wall.'

'Oh, it wasn't mad, only rather angry. And you did a splendid job of getting over that wall.'

'I couldn't have done it without your help. I—I'm very grateful.'

'It's good of you to say so after I've flung you over a wall, ruined your bonnet and made you lose most of your hairpins.'

She put her hand to her tumbled hair. 'Oh goodness, what a mess I must look!'

'Well you do, rather,' he said, looking at her critically. 'Can you tie up your hair with your scarf? Anyway, you have an excellent excuse for looking a mess. One's appearance does suffer when escaping an irritable bull in a narrow lane.'

Surprisingly, she found she could laugh. She managed to tie back her hair into some sort of order with the scarf. Thomas helped to brush off twigs and bits of grass from her coat and rescued the bonnet from a nearby bush. After which he made her take his arm and they set off through the shrubbery until they met a path.

As her shock wore off, she realised how Thomas's quick thinking and action in temporarily blinding the bull had saved them both from injury, or worse. She had every reason to be grateful to him, to the man who was a thief and who was found out, owing to her! The thought was, to say the least, deeply uncomfortable. And her discomfort grew stronger and more compelling as they came in sight of the house.

Should she warn him? But perhaps Alex had already confronted Thomas with the choice between returning the emeralds or prosecution. In fact Thomas must have given up the jewels or indicated where he had hidden them, if he were free to take a walk outside the estate. Had Alex told Thomas of her part in throwing suspicion on him? ·

Suspicion . . . *Was* Alex wrong and was Thomas guilty only of some silly prank?

'If I keep thinking and puzzling and worrying over it all,' she thought, 'I shall never say anything—and I think I *must*.'

'What is it?' Thomas asked as she stood still. 'Tired? It isn't far now. Hang on to me.'

'I've got to know,' she said quickly. 'Are you going to tell everyone who I am?'

'Good lord no, why should I? I can guess pretty accurately why you've done it and I still think it an absurd venture which will land you in trouble eventually. But if you need help you can call on me.'

This made things worse than ever!

'You already *have* helped me, I might have been killed,' she said unhappily. 'And—and I told Alex I saw you coming down from the balcony on the night of the ball, the night the necklace was stolen.'

He looked at her, his face telling her nothing. 'Did you? That's interesting.'

'Has Alex . . . been talking to you?' she asked hesitantly.

'Oh yes, he has.' He spoke absently, as if his thoughts were elsewhere.

She was suddenly reckless! She *had* to know.

'You came down from the balcony under Lady Grange's window, when everyone was downstairs. What were you doing there?'

For a moment she thought he had not heard her. His eyes had narrowed and the line of his mouth was hard. At last he said slowly,

'If I tell you, will you give me your word not to tell a soul?'

'I . . . very well, I promise,' she murmured.

'I was stealing Lady Grange's very beautiful emerald necklace,' he said, releasing her arm. 'I see the nurse and the boys coming, they'll take care of you. Bathe that hand and put some ointment on it.'

He swung around and walked away from her.

CHAPTER
ELEVEN

'TELL us again,' Mark begged, 'about the bull rushing at you! Were you *terribly* frightened, Annie?'

'*I* would have screamed and screamed,' Lucy said meditatively as she buried her small nose in her mug of cocoa.

'*I* would have jumped at the bull and hit him with my stick,' Giles boasted.

'I don't think Thomas had a stick,' his brother said. 'I bet you would have run away and the mad bull would have got you and trampled on you and—'

'That is enough, boys,' Vicky said sharply, so sharply that Sue glanced at her and then rose from the tea-table.

'I'm going to ask the housekeeper for some brandy,' she announced. 'You've had a rare fright and you're still shaky. Mercy, what an escape you've had! If Mr Craig hadn't of been there . . . You go to your room and have a lay down, I'll bring the brandy.'

Vicky obeyed meekly. She was in the grip of delayed shock and her hand was painful, and Thomas's confession still rang in her head. She tried to think clearly, but the brandy made her sleepy and she awoke, several hours later, feeling much refreshed and able to contemplate, with a calmer mind, Thomas's admission that he was the thief.

So Alex had been right. She had never been completely convinced of Thomas's guilt. His actions had been highly suspicious, but doubt had always lingered in her mind about him. Now that doubt no longer existed. He had confessed to stealing the necklace. But why had he told her? That remained yet another of the mysteries about Thomas Craig.

When she came out of her room she saw a figure hovering on the landing outside the nursery door.

'Oh, Nurse,' Mr Brett's face was suffused in a rosy blush, 'I—I heard something about your frightening experience this afternoon . . . an enraged bull in a narrow lane . . . You must have been in great danger, I fear. I—I thought I should come to enquire if you had recovered.'

She smiled at him. 'That is very kind of you, Mr Brett. It was not a pleasant experience, but Mr Craig's brave action saved us.'

'Indeed? I was not aware . . .'

'He flung his cape over the animal's head and helped me over a wall.'

'That was indeed very brave of him,' Mr Brett agreed. He shifted uneasily from one foot to the other before bursting out: 'How I wish *I* had been there to save you, Miss Annie! Although I fear I would not have had the nerve to do what he did.'

In which case, Vicky thought, he would not have been much use, but she was too kind to say it aloud. Instead, she said,

'I am quite recovered, sir. It was kind of you to ask.'

'Miss Annie, I leave Wellbury Court tomorrow afternoon, alas. Before I go, I wondered if—if there was a chance of my taking another photograph of you since I have lost the one I—'

'I'm sorry, but I'm really too busy,' Vicky said firmly, 'and you have the plate, you can always print another photograph.'

'But I haven't,' he exclaimed. 'It has gone! I really *cannot* think who has stolen both the study of you and Lucy *and* the plate.'

'Neither can I. I expect it was a joke and they will be returned to you before you leave,' she told him, a little impatiently, wishing he would not gaze at her with such soulful devotion. 'I really must go to the children.'

'Oh Miss Annie . . . may I not meet you—'

'Goodbye, Mr Brett,' she said kindly but firmly, and went to the nursery.

The house was in a bustle with departing guests, many of whom had been pleasurably intrigued by the novelty of a burglary during their visit and the prospect of telling their London friends about it. Maud sought Vicky that evening to say goodbye.

'Lady Grange leaves tomorrow and I am to go with her,' she said. 'I am quite glad, really. It has been so dreadfully upsetting, all this bother about the burglary and police and Lady Grange moaning and Effie's weeping.'

'Because of Alex Beaumont?'

'Well, yes. He's been so kind and says he'll meet her in London and that her mother will get over this silly idea he is after Effie's fortune.'

Vicky's slender brows drew together in a faint frown. 'I don't think he ought to let the poor girl imagine he has any serious intentions when he hasn't, it isn't kind.'

'Oh, but Effie seems to think he has. Of course he has not actually *said* anything, because her mother is so against him. Effie is not unhappy about *that*, but she is upset because her mother keeps scolding her, saying if Effie hadn't said the emeralds didn't go with the yellow dress, she would have worn the necklace that evening. And you know, she should not blame poor Effie altogether because it was Alex's suggestion that the emeralds would look wrong with . . . Oh dear!' Maud clasped her hands. 'I promised I wouldn't tell anyone! But I know you won't repeat it, Vicky. You see, it might make Lady Grange dislike Alex even more and then things would be more difficult than ever. I'm *so* glad Mama and Father could never find anything to dislike or disapprove of in dear Archie.'

Vicky said she was sure it must be a most comforting thought, and asked for news of her parents. Maud told her they had extended their visit in Boston with Harriet's in-laws-to-be. The society there, Lady Lynton had written, was very acceptable after the rigours of Montana.

During the rest of the day Vicky was fretted by a rising unrest and uneasiness. She must manage to contact Alex somehow. Unfortunately the weather was so bad she could not hope to meet him in the park or gardens. There would be no peace for her until she knew what had happened between Alex and Thomas, and how and where and when the emeralds would be returned to their owner. No doubt Thomas would find some excuse to leave Wellbury Court. Perhaps Alex was also planning to leave. As the hours passed and there was no message, her impatience swelled to a feverish determination to seek out Alex.

'If I could get a note to him,' she thought, 'but how? I can't trust anyone to take it, and anyway it would not be wise. I know he is in the blue room; if I could leave it there, when everyone is at dinner . . .'

The children were lively at bedtime and Sue unusually talkative. After supper, the housekeeper condescended to come and enquire if Vicky had recovered from her afternoon's experience, and it was late when Vicky managed to get away. The women would have left the dining-room and the men be settling down to their wine and cigars.

She sped swiftly down the stairs and across to the east wing. As she came to the landing she saw a man coming from the blue room and recognised Alex's valet. She was in the shadows and he did not notice her. When he had gone, she ran to the door and slipped into the room.

There was only one lamp burning and at first she did not see the man standing before the dressing-table. Then her heart lurched wildly and blood began to drum in her ears as she caught sight of Alex's face in the looking-glass, intent and gloating as he stared at something he held, something that slid through his fingers like green fire! He raised his head and their eyes met. He jerked around, staring.

'*Vicky!* What the devil . . .' his eyes went past her and he strode to the door and locked it, putting the key in his pocket. 'What in hell are you doing here?'

She was suddenly icy cold! Panic gripped her, then something inside her whispered: *Be careful!* Horror and fear sharpened her wits and she heard herself say in a near-normal voice,

'So you got the necklace from Thomas! How *clever* of you, Alex! Did he pretend he hadn't taken it or—or—'

He crossed the room and dropped the necklace into a drawer, then turned.

'You gave me a fright, my sweet Vicky,' he said lightly, but his eyes terrified her. 'I forgot to lock the door after my man left. It wouldn't do for someone to find me with the missing emeralds just yet, would it? Thomas gave them up after a struggle.' His eyes never left her and she fought to keep her expression one of excited interest. 'What made you come here?'

Her mouth was dry. 'I—I came to ask about Thomas. I wondered about . . . I was going to leave you a note. I must go back.'

'Not just yet, sweetheart, not until I've told you the plan I have for you—for us. I'm leaving here tomorrow and you are coming with me. We'll get married by special licence in London. You know I love you and I know you love me, dearest little Vicky. We'll be together for always, that is what you want, isn't it?'

She fought down her panic. 'Yes, oh yes of course it is, Alex. But so soon—'

'Darling,' he pulled her roughly into his arms,' I am taking you away from this wretched life. I've been in love with you since I first saw you. I love you—and I want you! Vicky, my dearest girl, no one knows we are here! We are alone. Let me love you, let me make you truly mine!'

'No!' She shrank away. 'No Alex, not—not here, not now! We shall be missed . . . someone will come. Of *course* I'll go with you tomorrow and—and marry you. Oh—I think I heard someone . . . I *must* go back! Please unlock the door, Alex!'

He let her go but stood watching her intently. 'I've decided to take the emeralds to London and send them anonymously to Lady Grange, she will think the thief has repented. Be at the first gate on the back avenue tomorrow morning and we'll drive up to London. I shall not let you remain here working like a servant. I'll meet you at ten-thirty. But you are to tell *no one*, do you understand? They will try to stop you.' He made a move to catch her in his arms again, but she eluded him, whispering,

'No, no, of course I won't say anything. But I must go now and pack my case and . . . Please open the door, Alex.'

She saw his eyes narrow and for a moment fear was ice in her veins. Then he went to the door and unlocked it and she fled back to the nursery.

Once in her own room, she sank onto the bed and faced the horror of her discovery. In that moment when she had seen Alex's face in the looking-glass the truth had burst upon her and she knew with certainty that Alex was the thief.

Shock held her rigid for some time, then slowly her mind awoke and she began to think clearly.

Alex must have taken the necklace when the ball was in progress. No one would have missed him in the time it would take him to get into the bedroom, either by way of the balcony or door. And who would suspect Alex Beaumont, handsome, well-born, popular and apparently wealthy? Lady Grange had discovered he was a gambler; was this how he paid his debts?

'And I helped him by suspecting Thomas,' she thought. 'He must have been amused! He must have enjoyed pretending he knew Thomas would do something like that, lying about him, and saying he would get the necklace from him. Alex never meant to return it. He's lied about everything!'

She shivered, thinking how close she had been to believing all his lies—and to loving him. Or had she?

She was too honest to deny the truth. 'I've been a silly, besotted fool, infatuated by an attractive man who amused himself pretending he was in love with me. I ought to have known the type of man he was by the way he treated poor Effie Grange. I thought it was all so romantic . . . seeing him at Devonshire House . . . meeting him here . . . meeting him secretly.'

Alex's charm, sensual and potent, had blinded her to all else. Her face burned as she remembered her response to his kisses and how he had haunted her thoughts and dreams. How easily he had fed her infatuation! What an innocent he must have thought her!

But she was not quite the innocent creature he thought her. She had hidden her shock and he believed she still thought Thomas the thief, and he was arrogantly sure she loved him. Instinct had given her the words and the power to deceive him.

What must she do now, denounce Alex? Who would believe her? And why did Alex wish to marry her now? She put her hands to her throbbing brow. Everything was in such a horrible *muddle*.

A flash of memory came: '. . . *an absurd venture which will land you in trouble eventually . . .*' Who had said that? *Thomas!*

She sprang to her feet, calling Sue.

'Go to James and tell him to get a message to Mr Craig that I want to see him immediately, Sue.'

Sue's mouth dropped open in horror. 'Eh, but the gentlemen are still at table and James—'

'This is very important, I'll explain later. Go,' she gave the girl a push. 'Do as I say—and *hurry*!'

She was pacing up and down the room, her nerves jumping, when the door opened and Thomas said,

'Something up?'

She ran to him. 'It's Alex! He stole the emeralds! He has them, but he pretends *you* stole them and says he will send them back to Lady Grange . . . and he is leaving tomorrow . . . and wants me to go with him and marry him . . .'

'Steady on,' Thomas took her arm and steered her into a chair and seated himself near her. 'How did you find out? Don't rush things, take your time and start at the beginning—when you lost your heart to Alex at Devonshire House.'

'I didn't—at least—' She paused to draw a deep breath, then began to speak, her words tumbling out in a frantic torrent.

When at last she faltered to a stop, he sat back, his hands in his pockets and his legs stretched out before him. He did not speak for some time, but she did not find the silence oppressive. She was feeling empty, and blessedly calm. Her fears seemed to have melted like snow before sunshine.

'I guessed, of course,' Thomas said, 'but I haven't been able to get proof. His luck broke—he's had amazing luck—when I got certain information from a man I defended who had been a receiver of stolen goods, jewels among them. I'd had a suspicion of Alex for some time. I knew his father had cut his allowance because of his gambling, but he always appeared to have money. I began to take an interest in his activities, especially in wealthy house-parties.'

'Did he know you suspected him?'

'I doubt it. He's enormously conceited with himself and his cleverness. And he was fairly safe, you know. Someone with his looks and background is pretty much beyond suspicion. He was helped by his attraction for women.' A quick, faintly ironic glance brought colour to her face. 'He's got poor little Effie madly in love with him; he probably planned to marry her and get his hands on her fortune.'

'He wants to marry *me*.'

'Sorry to spoil the romantic picture, but surely you know a wife can't be made to give evidence against her husband?'

'So that is why!' Vicky exclaimed indignantly. 'He pretended he was in love with me!'

'Oh, he probably was. You have a certain very compelling charm, Miss Vicky Lynton. Alex knew you would discover the truth about him sooner or later.' Thomas got up to go but Vicky said quickly,

'Wait; why did you pretend *you* were the thief?'

He shrugged. 'I didn't want anyone to suspect Alex just yet. Any more questions?'

'Yes. What were you doing coming down from the balcony that night?'

'Ah yes, that looked bad, didn't it? I'd seen Alex examining the balcony rather thoroughly on the pretext of testing its safety. I guessed he would try for the necklace on the night of the ball and might use the balcony so I decided to be in the bedroom when he came, but I was too late, the necklace had gone. I heard the maid coming and had to nip onto the balcony and as all the other windows were shut I had to shin down the vine. I knew Alex had been in the bedroom because he dropped a curious coin I knew he always carried as a sort of lucky charm. I dropped it—'

'And that was when I recognised you. Thomas, now you know Alex is the thief, what will you do?'

'We have already done it.'

'We?'

'The Inspector and I. Alex was still in his room. By the way, why did you visit him tonight?'

'I wanted to leave a note asking him to meet me sometime, I was feeling so tangled up about everything.'

'You should have come to me, I'm an excellent untangler. The Inspector has some questions he wants to ask Alex about the disappearance of other jewellery in country houses and Alex has thought it wiser to go with him to the station. The emeralds will be restored in due course and Effie can stop weeping.' He paused reflectively. 'I suppose she will start weeping for Alex now. If only these romantic females wouldn't fall in love so easily with handsome unscrupulous young men.'

She raised her chin defiantly. 'I suppose you mean me.'

'I mean you. You were on the point of losing your head over Alex. You were looking for romance when you thought up this little escapade.'

'I was *not*!' Her eyes sparkled angrily. 'I—I simply wanted to see a different side of life for a short while.'

'And you got yourself involved with a man who is a liar and a cheat. I suggest you retire from service, Miss Annie Fisher, tomorrow.'

'I shan't! You have no right to interfere!'

'All things considered, I think I have. I've had the trouble of keeping my eye on you, warning you about Alex, and saving you from a wrathful bull.'

'You had better think about your own situation,' she

told him sharply. 'How will you explain not telling the police before this about Alex? They will want to know why you took it upon yourself to keep him under surveillance. They may even suspect *you*.'

'I don't think so. My friend in Scotland Yard—he's rather high-up there—will tell them I worked under his orders. It has been easier for me to get invited to house-parties. I repeat, you had better leave Wellbury Court immediately, and if you refuse, I shall have to tell my hostess you are not suitable for the position you hold. May I suggest a dying aunt who is calling for you.'

She stared at him, speechless with indignation. At the door, he turned and she saw the laughter in his face and her eyes, green and furious, blazed at him as she cried,

'You are the most insufferable, infuriating man! I—I hope I never see you again.'

'I am sorry to disappoint you, Miss Lynton, but you will.'

'Why on earth should I?'

'Because you are going to marry me. Goodnight.'

CHAPTER
TWELVE

THE fire crackled softly in the grate. Outside, the wind blew a scatter of raindrops against the window. But Vicky heard nothing but the echo of Thomas's astounding words: 'You are going to marry me . . .'

He was mad, quite mad! What crazy notion had made him imagine such a fantastic thing could ever happen? Marry Thomas, who spent his time disapproving of her, scolding her, ordering her about . . .

Of course! He wanted to make her angry! He invariably aroused her to anger and it amused him! How often had she seen the lurking laughter in his blue eyes and his sudden, exasperating grin and smarted from them? He had deliberately chosen to say something he knew would make her forget her softened opinion of him. He was impossible, and she disliked him more than ever!

But he was dangerous because she knew he meant what he said about getting her dismissed if she did not give notice and leave Wellbury Court. It would be awkward for her, having to leave now, but she did not intend to let Thomas give her away or concoct some story about her that would mean her being ignominiously dismissed. Better to give notice, and as soon as possible.

When Sue came in, her face avid with curiosity, Vicky had her story ready. Her favourite aunt was housekeeper to Mr Craig and having heard her aunt was unwell, she had taken the liberty of asking Mr Craig how serious her aunt's illness was.

'Oh Sue, Mr Craig says she is quite *desperately* ill and she is asking for me!' Vicky produced a handkerchief and applied it to her eyes. 'I must go to her *at once!*'

'Oh laws, I'm right sorry, Annie. But what will you say to her ladyship? She'll be in a fine state at your leaving sudden-like . . . and you'll not be able to speak to her tonight, nor early tomorrow neither.'

Vicky had the answer to that. The events of the evening appeared to have sharpened her inventive gift to quite a remarkable degree.

'I shall leave a letter explaining everything. I expect she will promote you, Sue. You will make a splendid head nurse. I shan't be coming back, you see. I must nurse my poor aunt back to health if I can. Now be a dear girl and find Dumble and ask him to take me to the early train—and don't say a *word* to anyone, please.'

Sue went off, dazzled by her chance of promotion, and Vicky set about packing her few belongings, after which she wrote her letter to Lady Falconer. Sue returned with the time of the first train and Dumble's promise to have the dog-cart ready in the yard.

Vicky crept into the children's rooms for a silent farewell and felt a sudden sadness. She had become fond of them and knew they liked her and would miss her. Perhaps she would meet them in the park some day when Lady Falconer had taken up residence in her London house. Then she went to her room and sat on her bed and wondered what Great-Aunt Matilda was going to think when a rebel great-niece arrived on her doorstep.

It was cold and dark, with a ghostly dusting of frost on lawns and paths, when she crept down to the stableyard next morning and found Dumble harnessing the pony to the little dog-cart. He greeted her kindly and expressed sympathy for her aunt's condition.

'It's easy to see you've a soft heart,' he remarked as they drove down the back avenue under the latticework of bare trees now faintly outlined against the brightening sky. 'I'm not saying but her ladyship may take offence at you slipping off secret-like, her having lost Nurse Brodmin and all.'

'But you do see I *have* to go, don't you, Dumble? She is my favourite aunt and I must go to her at once—before it is too late!'

'We'll hope for the best, Missie. The children will miss you sorely.'

The pony's hoofs rang sharply on the frozen ground. The sky took on a misty veil of pale rose that slowly deepened to apricot and then merged into vivid gold heralding the sun's arrival. Vicky sat silently, gripping her case, her eyes on the awakening sky as memories flooded her mind.

Alex, with whom she had so nearly fallen in love and whose career as a popular, leisured young society bachelor was over. Lady Falconer, pretty and petulant and soon to be extremely angry with her ex-nurse. The big house holding its two worlds, upstairs and downstairs, each with such a limited knowledge of the other.

Her attempt to break away from her life of a débutante had not been at all what she had supposed. And it *had* ended in trouble—as Thomas had predicted.

Thomas!

'I refuse to think about him,' she told herself with great firmness. 'He is the most tiresome person I have ever known. However, I don't suppose I shall see him again.'

To her chagrin, this thought did not bring all the satisfaction she had expected. And it was not so easy to stop thinking about Thomas. He intruded upon her thoughts in a most irritating way, probably because he had annoyed her on so many occasions and—she admit-

ted reluctantly—because he had seen through her infatuation with Alex and predicted disillusion.

She had plenty of time in which to think of the
problems ahead of her, after she had taken a friendly
farewell of Dumble and started on her long journey.

Did she regret taking Lizzie's place at Wellbury
Court? There had certainly been plenty of incident
during her time there, but memories of Alex Beaumont
remained painful. She had very nearly made a fool of
herself over him and the memory rankled when she
thought of Thomas's warning . . .

What with changing trains, and a long wait in London
for a train north, it was late in the evening when Vicky,
chilled and deeply weary, arrived in the town nearest
Bracken Manor, her aunt's home, where she managed
to hire a rickety carriage to take her on the last lap of her
journey.

The door was opened by an elderly butler who stared
at her in disapproval when she asked for her aunt.

'Mrs Pendred is about to retire, miss.'

'Well I must see her, please. Tell her it is her niece,
Miss Victoria Lynton.'

He looked even more disapproving, but allowed her
to enter and showed her into a room where the remains
of a fire glowed in the grate. She went to it, swamped by
a sudden, dismaying thought that perhaps this was the
most unwise thing she had yet done. Her aunt had said
she might come to her if she was ever in need of help, but
what would she think of a niece who had told lies and
deceived her parents and demeaned herself by working
as a nursemaid? Girls, nice girls, did not behave in this
way. Her aunt would probably think her fast and 'one of
these modern creatures' and refuse to condone her
behaviour.

She was wondering drearily why she had ever thought
of taking shelter in Norfolk when the door opened and

the Honourable Mrs Pendred, magnificently regal in purple satin dressing-gown, lace cap with green ribbons and a disgraceful pair of tartan slippers, entered.

'So here you are,' was her greeting, which did nothing to raise Vicky's rapidly sinking spirits. 'I wondered how long it would take you to get into trouble when your parents left you. What have you been up to, young woman? Wait,' she held up an imperious hand as Vicky began to speak. 'You look frightful. Where did you get those clothes? Are you hungry?'

'Yes, very hungry indeed, Aunt Matilda.'

'Ring that bell. You look half dead. Where have you come from?'

'Devonshire.'

'My God! Ransome,' she turned to the butler who had entered,' some soup and sandwiches—and a glass of burgundy.'

'Very well, Madam.' Ransome withdrew, managing to convey his increasing disgust at the proceedings.

'I'm afraid Ransome doesn't approve of me,' Vicky sighed.

'He enjoys disapproving, it's his hobby. That's why he remains with me, I keep him supplied with material. Sit down child and don't try to talk until you've eaten something. I think I'll get Ransome to bring me some wine too, I've a feeling I may need it.'

The food put new life into Vicky and the wine warmed her chilled body and brought a flush to her cheeks and fresh courage to carry off what might be a ticklish situation.

'Now,' her aunt said when Ransome had taken the tray away, 'begin. You are in some sort of a pickle, that is easily seen. What have you been up to?'

'I have been working as a children's nurse at Wellbury Court, Sir Charles Falconer's home.'

Her aunt stared, then drained her glass of wine. 'I

knew I'd need that. Now, begin at the beginning, and don't tell any more lies.'

Surprise made Vicky ask: 'How do you know I have told lies?'

'Your mother wrote from America to ask if I would mind extending your visit as she was enjoying Boston society and was not returning immediately. Andrew doesn't care for society, but he's had to agree after dragging her across the Atlantic to look at a lot of old bones. I've been expecting you. Well?'

The fire had been resurrected—unwillingly—by Ransome and the room was pleasantly warm. Vicky felt a great desire to sleep come over her as she began her account of her visit to Wellbury Court and her experiences there.

Mrs Pendred listened without interrupting. From time to time she pushed her lace cap farther back, revealing a row of curl-papers. When Vicky had finished there was a silence in which the room began to swim gently around her as the longing for sleep became overpowering. Her aunt's voice woke her from her near-dreaming state.

'I guessed you were doing something ridiculous which your parents wouldn't like, which was why I didn't answer your mother's letter. You have behaved in the most disgraceful and irresponsible way. You have deceived your parents and told a perfectly amazing number of lies and got yourself nicely tangled up with a handsome young criminal. I suppose you thought it all very romantic and decided to fall in love with him.'

'Well—yes, I'm afraid I did.'

'You have been *wildly* rash. He might have seduced you.'

'He did say he wanted to marry me . . .'

'Well we know why *that* was, and no compliment to you. The only person who seems to have had any sense is this man called Thomas Craig.'

Vicky looked up quickly. 'I would rather not speak of him.'

'After he made you lose your temper, and threw you over a wall and saved your life? Nonsense, of course you'll think of him! I like the sound of him, who is he?'

'He is a barrister . . . and I would love to go to bed, Aunt Matilda.' She had taken care *not* to mention Thomas's last, astounding words!

'Yes, you are half asleep already.' Mrs Pendred rose, gathering her purple gown around her. 'Tomorrow we shall go shopping. I refuse to allow you to wear those frightful clothes a minute longer. Come with me, the spare room is ready.'

As soon as her head touched the pillow, Vicky was enveloped in a deep and dreamless sleep. She awoke to see a maid placing a breakfast tray on the bedside table. The curtains were drawn and a thin, primrose-pale sunlight filled the room, striking prismatic gleams from the array of cut glass on the dressing-table and crystal candle-holders on the mantlepiece. A fire burned cheerfully in the grate and there was solid comfort in the big walnut wardrobe and chest of drawers and handsomely framed reproduction of the Burne-Jones painting 'King Cophetua and the Beggar-Maid' which, Vicky hoped, argued a leaning towards romance in her aunt's nature.

A hip-bath was placed on a towel before the fire and filled with hot water. When she had bathed and dressed, Vicky made her way to the morning room where she found her aunt at her writing desk.

Mrs Pendred laid down her pen and turned. 'You look better than you did last night, I will say that. Anything more like a drowned kitten I have yet to see. No need to ask if you slept well. I have had a letter from your sister Flora who says she expects your parents in ten days time. Maud is with her and appears to have held her tongue about you. *That* may get the poor girl into trouble with your mother and father, have you thought about that?'

'Yes, I have. I shall explain how I persuaded her to keep silent. Aunt Matilda, are you going to tell Mama and Father about my time at Wellbury Court?'

'I have not made up my mind about that yet.'

'Well I've made up *my* mind. I shall tell them *everything.*'

Her aunt subjected her to a long, thoughtful stare.

'I rather thought you would,' she said at last. 'You don't lack courage. Your father will forgive you, of course, and your mother will go into near-hysterics and lecture you for weeks. You had better get back into her good graces by marrying some man with money and a title. Your mother won't have a restful moment until she has got you safely married.'

'I have no intention of marrying anyone, least of all a title, thank you Aunt Matilda.'

'Nonsense! You'll be married soon, and most probably to that Thomas who threw you over a wall.'

Vicky dropped into a chair. 'That is the very last thing—'

'He sounds sensible,' her aunt continued, ignoring her, 'A man who thinks as quickly as that and who likes you enough to warn you when you are about to make a fool of yourself, is the man for you, Vicky.'

'He isn't! And he doesn't like me.'

'Rubbish! He is probably in love with you by now, in spite of the way you have behaved. Now don't start spluttering, Vicky. You go as red as a beetroot when the man's name is mentioned. Get your coat and that frightful bonnet. Jock is bringing the carriage around and we will drive into town.'

Vicky obeyed meekly, since there was nothing else she could do. Her aunt did not mention Thomas again, for which she was grateful. Her feelings about Thomas were becoming complicated and she wished to forget them, and him, as soon as possible.

They returned to Bracken Manor laden with parcels and Vicky was ordered to hand over her nurse's clothes to be given to the deserving poor. When she had changed into her new dress, rose velvet with tucked net under-blouse, she surveyed herself in the looking-glass with satisfaction. The colour gave a faint glow to her creamy skin. She thought, critically, that she had seldom looked better. Her eyes, a luminous silvery-green between the thick, curling lashes, had a brilliance that made them beautiful; and her hair, charmingly arranged by her aunt's maid, made her smile as she recalled her battles with hairnet and hairpins.

'Farewell, Annie Fisher,' she told her reflection. 'Welcome back, the last Miss Lynton!'

She glanced at the pretty beaded slippers, fine kid boots, fur-trimmed coat and chic little fur toque her aunt had bought her. She was back in her comfortable, easy, well-dressed life where, within reason, she could have what she wished in the way of material comforts. A richly luxurious life compared with the life Annie Fisher had led, and one she had more than once thought of rather longingly when she had been immured in the Falconer nursery with only Sue for company.

Everything was going to turn out all right. Her parents would scold, but forgive her eventually, as her aunt had predicted. Probably they would think her experiences would prevent her from ever trying such a thing again. Possibly they would be right.

She turned away from the glass abruptly. If everything was going to be all right, why was she beset by a restive feeling that all was *not* right?

'It's reaction,' she told herself as she went down to join her aunt for tea. 'It will take a little time to adjust after all that has happened at Wellbury Court. I will soon stop thinking about it.'

She had already stopped thinking about Alex. He had become a shadowy figure and even the memory of the revelation of guilt she had surprised in his handsome face was fading, together with the shock of knowing the truth about him. He had gone out of her life as abruptly as he had entered it. Her aunt's only comment on Alex was that he must have had a shocking upbringing and she had heard the Beaumonts were an odd family.

She decided she would send Sue a present, gloves or perhaps silk stockings, and a warm woollen scarf to Dumble, and presents to the children. She felt pretty sure Lady Falconer would not recognise her late nurse if she should meet Miss Victoria Lynton in her elegant clothes at some society function. As with many of her type, those she employed were faceless machines who left no imprint upon her mind.

Mrs Pendred was comfortably ensconced before the fire with the toes of her slippers on the fender. The day, bright at first, had changed and a fine sleet was blurring the windows as the butler drew the thick velvet curtains.

'Put the crumpets down by the fire, Ransome,' Mrs Pendred ordered, 'I detest a lukewarm crumpet.'

'As you wish, Madam.' Ransome did as she ordered, his manner conveying his opinion that the place for the crumpet dish was on the table.

'You can pour out the tea, Vicky, and give me one of those crumpets. Ransome thinks crumpets are vulgar, he prefers the horrid little tea-cakes cook makes. I want to hear more about Wellbury Court and who was there. I have met Lady Falconer, a pretty woman without much brain—not that her husband has much of a brain either. Were the children stupid?'

'No, they were charming and I became very fond of them,' Vicky told her as she picked up the heavy silver teapot. 'Lady French was among the visitors—'

'A wicked old gossip. I wonder she did not recognise you, she has a most unfortunately retentive memory, it is why she is so unpopular.'

'She did say I reminded her of someone. Lady Grange and her daughter, Effie, were there of course. Do you know them?'

'No. The girl is an heiress, isn't she? If Beaumont had married her he would not have had to steal people's jewels for a living.'

'Maud said Effie was fond of him, but her mother didn't approve of him because he gambled.'

'Was the ball very grand? No expense spared, I suppose. Lady Falconer is all for show, like all silly women. Did you feel you wanted to be at the ball instead at looking at it from ouside?'

Vicky handed her aunt her cup of tea. 'Well, yes I did, I'm afraid. It was a truly magnificent ball and the music set my toes tingling. I suppose that was why I went to have another peep.'

'And caught young Thomas scrambling down from a balcony outside Lady Grange's bedroom,' Mrs Pendred bit into a dripping crumpet with relish. 'Of course it looked as if he had taken the emeralds, but I would have thought you had sense enough to know he wasn't the type of man to be a sneak-thief.'

'I was very surprised,' Vicky admitted, 'but I didn't know him well. And Alex told me things about him—'

'A pack of clever lies calculated to set you against his so-called friend. You know, I have some admiration for Beaumont, he's a rascal but a clever one. He didn't mind taking risks and that shows courage. But how you could have been silly enough to be taken in by a handsome face . . .'

Vicky sat up, her back very straight and a glint in her eyes.

'I believe *you* were once taken in by a handsome young tutor and actually ran away with him, Aunt Matilda.'

Her aunt spilt some of her tea. 'Now look what you have made me do! Who on earth told you . . . Well if I did, I soon realised my mistake and was extremely glad when my father followed us and brought me home.'

'I have realised my mistake also. Would you like another cup of tea?'

Vicky was enjoying herself. There was an abrasive quality about her aunt that appealed to her and after the web of lies in which she had involved herself, it was refreshing to hear and be able to speak the truth.

Of course the truth about Alex had been a shock. The truth about Thomas . . . No, that had not been a shock. Subconsciously she had known he was not guilty. But she certainly had *not* known he had this crazy idea of marrying her! But of course she had already decided that he meant only to annoy her. He was the most persistently annoying man she had ever known—and she would *not* continue to think about him!

'You've gone pink and your eyes are green,' her aunt remarked. 'I suppose you are thinking about that man, Thomas. Does he know you are here?'

'Of course not, I didn't tell anyone where I was going.'

'Well if he wants you, he will find you. Of course, you may have put him off by the way you have behaved. Once he thinks seriously of how you let yourself be taken in by an attractive wastrel he may well have second thoughts about you.'

'I most sincerely hope he will!' Vicky said vehemently, 'and it's the fire that is making my face pink, Aunt Matilda!'

CHAPTER
THIRTEEN

VICKY wrote to Maud to tell her she had found shelter with Aunt Matilda. Maud's return letter was one of obvious relief and approval and the somewhat forlorn hope that their parents might not react in too disastrous a manner when their youngest daughter revealed her most undutiful behaviour.

'*I* won't say anything, of course,' Maud wrote, 'but I think you are *quite* right to tell Mama and Father the truth. I fear they may not be pleased, but I shall tell them you did not do anything *shocking* and were shut up in the nursery most of the time.'

'But not all the time, unfortunately,' was Mrs Pendred's remark when Vicky showed her the letter. 'I never would have believed Maud could keep silent about something for so long. She isn't as silly as she looks.'

'Aunt Matilda, Maud doesn't look silly,' Vicky protested.

'All your sisters are beautiful little ninnies who will make excellent wives and mothers and never give parents or husbands a moment's anxiety,' her aunt pronounced. 'The man I'm sorry for is that Thomas. He'll have to keep his eye on you.'

'Isn't that one way to keep a husband interested?' Vicky asked. 'Not that I have the least intention of marrying Thomas Craig, even if he asks me—which of course he won't.'

'Which is just as well,' Mrs Pendred said surprisingly.

They were sitting in the window of the morning room with the pale winter sunshine falling on Vicky's dark curls and pensive face. 'He wouldn't do for you.'

'I thought you said he would,' Vicky exclaimed.

'I've changed my mind. If you keep falling in love with handsome—I believe you said Thomas was plain?—attractive young men with peculiar methods of earning a living, you had better marry one. I imagine you will not have much trouble finding one in the vortex of today's society. Thomas is much too prosaic for you.'

'But he isn't prosaic . . . and I never said he was plain. He has a—rather square, *chunky* face and very blue eyes and straight, dark brows and—'

'Well, you had better forget him. I am taking you to lunch with the Fosters, they have a house-party of young people and you can forget about emeralds and Alex Beaumont's kisses—of course he kissed you and made you think he meant it—and all the nonsense and trouble you kicked up for yourself in Devonshire. Wear that rose dress, it suits you. The Foster boy has an eye for pretty girls.'

But in the days following Vicky had little luck in dismissing memories. They invaded her dreams and hovered at the back of her mind to appear with startling suddenness at most unexpected moments, even obliterating her speculations on how her parents would receive her confession.

Mrs Pendred had announced her intention of accompanying her niece to London, to see the fun, she declared, but Vicky knew, with a rush of warm affection, that it was an unacknowledged wish to pour oil on troubled waters, if anything so soothing as oil could be associated with Aunt Matilda.

The days passed peacefully in drives around the country, shopping, tea-parties and visits to neighbours, but Vicky was not peaceful. She had a bleak feeling that her life had been emptied of meaning and the future was a dreary prospect she did not wish to dwell upon. She continued to assure herself it was to be expected after the dramatic end to her existence as Annie Fisher, and continued to believe it less as her return to London drew nearer.

At last the day came when the carriage was ordered to take her and her aunt to the station, after Ransome had gloomily predicted a possible railway accident—his face suggested a fatal one—and the certainty of a dangerous chill caused by travelling in bad weather.

'You would think the man *wanted* me to meet my death,' Mrs Pendred snorted as the carriage bore them away. 'Actually, he would be perfectly lost if he did not have me to disapprove of.'

The journey proved comfortable and without accident or danger of a chill. In the cab that drove them to the Lynton residence, Vicky looked up to see her aunt's eyes fixed on her.

'D'you feel nervous at meeting your mother and father?' she demanded abruptly. 'If they take too strong a line with you, you can come back with me to Bracken Manor. You've behaved extremely, badly, but I won't let them break your spirit.'

Impulsively, Vicky kissed her aunt's cheek. 'You're a darling, Aunt Matilda, and I love you! With you beside me I can face anything.'

Her aunt grunted in a noncommittal manner, but she was smiling as the cab drew up.

Vicky had written a short note to her mother to say when she and Aunt Matilda would be arriving. Lady Lynton and Sir Andrew were in the library when the butler showed the arrivals in. Lady Lynton rose and embraced her daughter and, with less enthusiasm, her aunt. Sir Andrew kissed Vicky and then held her back, looking at her critically as he remarked,

'Norfolk appears to agree with you, Vicky. You look blooming. You are looking well too, Matilda.'

'Thank you, Andrew. But I am in dire need of some tea, and so is Vicky. We have had a long journey. How did the Montana trip go?'

'Magnificently!' Sir Andrew began to pace up and down. 'I wouldn't have missed it for worlds! This new find of the jawbone of—'

'Ring for tea, Andrew dear,' his wife interrupted. 'It was rather *primitive*, you know, and most of the people we met were quite unable to speak of anything but those odd bones and how ancient they were, though I never can understand how they *know*. It was *quite* different in Boston. Such pleasant society, really quite like England, you know. I was surprised.'

'You mean they weren't wearing home-spun clothes and chewing tobacco?' Mrs Pendred asked as she pulled off her gloves. 'Well, you've learned something. Travel broadens the mind, they say. Ah, here comes tea. I hope it is strong, Elizabeth.'

At her mother's request, Vicky attended to the tea-table while her aunt listened somewhat abstractedly to the account of Maud's engagement to Lord Burnley.

'So she has caught him at last,' she remarked, rolling up her veil. 'Well, I consider she deserves him. She's a girl who can hold her tongue when necessary.'

'I am sure dear Maud has never had reason to keep anything hidden from us,' Lady Lynton said reproachfully. 'All my girls are perfectly open with us.'

'Except your last one.' Mrs Pendred swallowed a piece of walnut cake, drained her teacup and sat back. 'You had better start, Vicky, and get it over.'

Vicky drew a deep breath, glanced at her aunt, and was suddenly filled with reckless courage as she plunged into her story of how she had spent her time while her loving and deceived parents were in America.

Lady Lynton's charming face slowly paled and her eyes began to protrude and her mouth to make nervous movements as if words were struggling to burst forth.

Sir Andrew, after a searching look at his youngest child, stood in front of the fire with his hands in his pockets and a deepening frown on his face.

It took some time, but no one interrupted the tale of a rebellious daughter's disappearance into the character of Annie Fisher, nurse to the Falconer family in Devonshire. The actual recovery of the emeralds was glossed over and the Lyntons left with a hazy idea that the thief was a slightly dubious character who had slipped into the house-party by reason of his charm. That was how Vicky wished it to remain, but she reckoned without her aunt's sense of the dramatic—and an unholy desire to see some fun!

'He was Alex Beaumont,' she declared, slipping her furs off her shoulders, 'old Beaumont's younger son, a gambler who gambled with money from his booty. Been suspected for some time, it appears. A bad lot, and dangerously attractive to romantic young women.'

'Old Beaumont's son?' Sir Andrew burst out. 'Good lord! I'd heard he played pretty near the wind, and hadn't a particularly savoury reputation with . . .' he stopped and glanced at his wife and daughter.

'With women,' Mrs Pendred finished composedly. 'You need not be discreet, Andrew. Vicky knows all about him; she fell in love with him.'

'*What?*' The word burst simultaneously from Lady Lynton and Sir Andrew.

Vicky looked reproachfully at her aunt, she had not thought her capable of such treachery. But Aunt Matilda was enjoying herself far too much to be disturbed by a niece's accusing glance.

'She succumbed to his undoubted charm and became persuaded she loved him madly. Luckily the shock of discovering him to be a criminal had the effect of destroying the illusion, and now she has other plans.'

Poor Lady Lynton raised a feeble hand to her brow. 'I—I simply cannot understand how Vicky could have wished to lower herself by becoming a servant—'

Her husband interrupted her impatiently. 'No honest work is low, but what I cannot condone is the way she lied to us; that story of staying in Norfolk all the time we were to be in America!'

'I wrote to Aunt Matilda before we left,' Lady Lynton moaned, 'thanking her for inviting Vicky to stay. Didn't she get the letter?'

'No, she didn't,' Vicky said, 'I threw it away.' A strange calm had descended upon her. They knew the worst and now it was up to them to decide what the punishment would be. It must be the calmness of despair, she thought, which was giving her this serene feeling.

'I simply cannot understand,' her mother reiterated in a voice of despair, 'how a child of mine could be so dreadfully deceitful and behave in so—so wild a manner! If Vicky really wished for some type of work, there are charitable institutions—'

'Where she could spend her time sewing drawers for the ungodly heathen who are much healthier without them,' Mrs Pendred said. 'Now, be sensible, Elizabeth, and realise all young people want to kick over the traces once in a while.'

'*I* never did, and none of the other girls ever did.'

'Well no, they didn't. But what about Andrew? *He* wanted to go on the stage when he was young and did a season in a Drury Lane pantomime and fell in love with the fairy queen.'

Sir Andrew gave a start. 'How in God's name did you know . . . However, that has nothing to do with this.' He glared at Mrs Pendred. 'Vicky has behaved extraordinarily naughtily and she should be made to see—'

'Andrew, did you *really* perform in a pantomime?' Lady Lynton demanded.

'Of course he did,' her aunt told her. 'Probably as the hind legs of an elephant, or Dick Whittington's cat.'

'I was third robber in Babes in the Wood,' Sir Andrew was goaded into admitting, 'and I wish to goodness, Matilda, you would mind your own business! I believe you encouraged Vicky in this nonsense. I shall give the matter some thought, and decide what to do about Vicky.'

Mrs Pendred settled herself comfortably in her chair and stretched out her toes to the fire.

'She's decided for herself. She is going to marry a man called Thomas Craig who threw her over a wall and saved her life.'

Vicky's hands flew to her scarlet cheeks while her parents stared at her in speechless amazement. Before anyone could speak, the door opened and the butler announced,

'Mr Thomas Craig.'

He paused in the doorway, surveying the transfixed group around the tea-table in mild surprise. Mrs Pendred was the first to recover. She sat up and bowed her head with its violet-trimmed toque and spotted veil in a gracious and well-born manner.

'Good afternoon, Mr Craig. We have not met, but my niece has spoken your name more than once. I believe you met in Devonshire?'

Thomas bowed. 'Yes, I had that pleasure. I must apologise for this intrusion.'

'No need to, Mr Craig. Vicky will perform the introductions.'

Vicky swallowed and rose, her legs feeling oddly weak. 'Aunt Matilda, Mama, Father, this is Mr Craig whom I met when I was at Wellbury Court.'

Lady Lynton remained speechless but her husband bent a frowning eye on the visitor.

'Where my daughter was masquerading as a nurse, Mr Craig?'

'It was no masquerade, Sir Andrew. Miss Lynton proved to be a most excellent nursemaid and was promoted to the position of head nurse in no time.'

'Then you were aware of my daughter's true identity?'

'Yes, I was. I recognised her.'

'And you did not consider it your duty to inform Lady Falconer?'

'No.' Thomas met Sir Andrew's frowning glance with no sign of guilt. 'For all I knew, Sir Andrew, it might have been with your consent that Miss Lynton chose to experience another side of social life.'

'Good heavens, man, do you think I'd have allowed her to become a servant looking after someone's brats?'

'No honest work is low,' Mrs Pendred observed, 'you said so yourself, Andrew. I must ask you to sit down, Mr Craig, since at the moment Lady Lynton is too overcome to do so. Ring for fresh tea, Vicky. How did you leave Sir Charles and Lady Falconer?'

'Recovering.' Thomas seated himself after Lady Lynton had inclined her head faintly in his direction. 'Miss Lynton will have told you of the unfortunate occurrences in the household and the anxiety everyone felt until the Grange emerald necklace had been recovered.'

'Stolen by old Beaumont's son,' Sir Andrew growled. 'Hard to believe, but there's always been a funny streak in the Beaumonts. I remember when an uncle . . . Well it doesn't matter. Nasty thing to happen at a ball.'

Lady Lynton had been gazing at Thomas in growing bewilderment. Suddenly she said,

'Why did you throw my daughter over a wall, Mr Craig?'

'There was a mad bull and we were in a narrow lane

and I would have been gored and probably killed if Thomas—if Mr Craig hadn't boosted me over a wall and saved me,' Vicky said. She was sitting upright with her hands folded in her lap, her chin raised and her eyes very green. 'May I ask why you have paid us a visit, Mr Craig?'

'Of course. Your sister told me you were expected today and I called to ask how you were after your journey.'

'Very right and proper,' Mrs Pendred remarked. 'Here is the fresh tea. Vicky will give you some as her mother is still suffering from shock. Vicky has just revealed all, you see. I am glad you came, Mr Craig, the atmosphere was becoming a trifle strained and moral precepts on the duties of children to their parents about to be expressed.'

Lady Lynton was roused to protest. 'I consider we have every right to expect dutiful behaviour in our daughters! Vicky has behaved extremely foolishly—'

'Yes, yes,' her husband interposed impatiently, 'we've gone into that. No need to tell the world about it.'

'And no need to tell Mr Craig,' Mrs Pendred said, 'he, too, knows all. I'll have some more tea, Vicky. You don't make your tea strong enough, Elizabeth. I suppose this washy stuff is fashionable. Must you go, Mr Craig?'

'Yes, Mrs Pendred.'

'But you will call again, I hope?'

Thomas glanced at Vicky who refused to meet his eyes.

'I should like to.'

'I shall not be here,' Vicky said quickly, 'I'm going back to Norfolk with my aunt.'

'You are doing nothing of the kind,' her father snapped. 'You're staying where I can keep an eye on you, my girl. Lord knows what mad idea you may get next.'

'Getting work in a pantomime,' Mrs Pendred sug-

gested, waving her lorgnette, 'as a fairy queen, perhaps.'
Sir Andrew's furious glare did nothing to discompose
her. 'It is better Vicky should remain in London, Mr
Craig. You are a busy man and Norfolk is a long way
from London.'

Thomas's eyes narrowed in sudden laughter. 'Thank
you, Mrs Pendred. I am very happy to have made your
acquaintance.'

He bowed, took formal farewell of Lady Lynton and
Sir Andrew, and withdrew, leaving a faintly stunned
silence behind him.

Lady Lynton spoke first. 'I do not understand. I
simply do *not* understand *anything* about all this.' She
looked appealingly at her husband who was staring
thoughtfully into the fire, but she got no help from him.
Sir Andrew raised his head to stare at his daughter for
some minutes, then returned to his contemplation of the
leaping flames and silence fell once more.

Vicky was in her bedroom, sitting before the dressing-
table while her mother's maid brushed her hair, when
her aunt entered. Her visit was not a surprise; Vicky had
expected it. She dismissed the maid and invited her aunt
to sit down.

'Is your room all right, Aunt Matilda? Are you comfortable?'

'As comfortable as a woman of my age ever is in
someone else's house. I do not admire these French
paintings. I do not consider the one in my room suitable
for a bedroom, the young woman is only half dressed.'

'I would have thought a bedroom was the best place
for her. I'm sure if you could have asked Monet—'

'Stop twittering, Vicky.' Mrs Pendred extended her
feet, revealing the disgraceful tartan slippers. 'I like your
young man.'

'He isn't my young man.'

'Not yet, and he may never be if you go on in this idiotic way. Some more discerning girl will snap him up. He is an extremely attractive young man with more character than I have learned to expect from modern young men. Has he asked you to marry him?'

'No.' Thomas's outrageous declaration could by no means be considered a proposal. 'And I don't want him to. I don't dislike him, and I am very grateful to him for saving me from that bull, but that is all. I can't imagine why he called this afternoon, I'm sure Mama and Father thought it strange.'

Her aunt snorted inelegantly. 'After what you told them, nothing could seem strange. I came to say that if your parents object to your marrying Thomas, you can come to me and be married from my house. However,' she gathered the purple dressing-gown around her as she rose, 'if you are not going to marry him, there is no problem. Goodnight, I hope you will sleep well.'

Vicky hoped so too, but her wish was unfulfilled. Sleep did not come for a long time, during which time she thought of Thomas. She did not want to; she had not meant to. She tried without success to stop thinking about him. Had he, *could* he, have been serious when he said she was going to marry him? Vicky turned restlessly on her pillow. She had decided he merely meant to annoy her. But if he *did* mean it . . . He had never shown the least sign of falling in love with her, in fact he disapproved of her and thought she was a silly little infatuated fool.

'Which I was,' she admitted. 'I wish he hadn't come. He sat there, looking so—so confident! And Father liked him, I could see that, and Mama didn't dislike him. Of course Aunt Matilda merely wants to get me married to someone so I shan't get into trouble again.'

If Thomas was, by some fantastic chance, in love with her, he had showed no signs of it. He had never tried to meet her secretly in the gardens, or turned up when she took the children for a walk in the park. He had certainly never paid her any compliments, or tried to kiss her . . .

Her heart gave a jolt that made her gasp with dismay. Why should the idea of Thomas kissing her set her pulse racing?

'I hope I'll never see him again! I—I'll tell them to say I'm not at home! I'll go and stay with Flora . . . I will not be bullied into marrying Thomas Craig!'

CHAPTER
FOURTEEN

Mrs Pendred declared that since she had to be in London she might as well see what it offered and Vicky, still under suspended sentence, was ordered to take her about as Lady Lynton did not feel up to it.

Rather to Vicky's surprise, no more was said about her escapade, but whether this was owing to a need to assess her disobedience and depths of her deception, or her aunt's intervention, was not obvious and she could only hope for the best.

It soon became plain that Mrs Pendred derived most satisfaction from disapproving of what she saw, and Vicky took a wicked pleasure in taking her to an exhibition of French impressionist paintings. Her aunt's reactions were all she had foreseen.

'Disgusting! Revolting!' Mrs Pendred waved her lorgnette at the painting before her. 'Indecent! A naked hussy! You can tell *her* trade by the look on her face! Disgraceful!'

At this, several people near looked at Mrs Pendred a little nervously and moved away.

'But Manet got beautiful flesh tones—'

'I see nothing beautiful in a shameless hussy laid out like a fish on a fishmonger's slab,' Mrs Pendred announced in ringing tones that drew even more attention to her. She moved on, like a majestic ship in full sail, her grey velvet coat surmounted with a sable stole from which dangled a succession of little fur paws which,

Vicky thought with inward laughter, might at any minute be raised in horror as great as their owner's. The very quills in her hat seemed to quiver with indignation.

She paused to stare at a Gauguin. Vicky awaited a salvo of disapproval but all her aunt said was: 'Poor creature, obviously deranged,' before turning to announce she needed her tea and they would at once proceed to Gunter's.

Once in the discreetly luxurious atmosphere of the famous tea-shop with its green walls, cream paint, palms, and waitresses in caps with streamers, Mrs Pendred relaxed and ordered strong tea and cream éclairs.

'Have your parents said anything further about your life as a nursemaid?' she asked, drawing off her grey kid gloves.

'No, they haven't. I've been expecting them to,' Vicky told her.

'I haven't. Your mother moulds her opinions on Andrew's and he can't make up his mind about you yet. You are uncomfortably like him in character and that does make things difficult for him.'

'You mean about the pantomime? That was naughty of you, Aunt Matilda. Was he very much in love with the fairy queen?'

Her aunt chuckled. 'For the run of the pantomime. She had the most improbable golden hair and a husband who was a plumber. By the way, if you wish to blush, do it now, before Mr Thomas Craig observes it and jumps to the conclusion he is the cause.'

Vicky turned quickly. Thomas was standing in the doorway surveying the room. He saw them and smiled and after hanging his hat on the hat-stand, made his way leisurely through the little tables and hurrying waitresses.

Vicky was forced to admit London clothes suited him;

he looked well in the grey coat and striped trousers. She turned to her aunt with determined coolness.

'I suppose he is meeting someone here.'

'Good afternoon, Mrs Pendred,' Thomas bowed, 'and Miss Lynton.'

'Join us, please,' Mrs Pendred said, to Vicky's dismay.

'I shall be delighted to,' he said and sat down opposite Vicky who said hastily,

'We are about to leave—'

'Nonsense, I haven't begun on my second éclair yet,' Mrs Pendred remarked and turned to Thomas. 'My cook cannot make them and the shop ones taste of card-board. They are one of the two reasons why I am in London.'

'May I ask what is the other?'

'To keep an eye on my niece, the last one.' She licked a spot of cream off her finger and looked across the room. 'Good heavens, there is old Lady Oxwell! I thought she was dead. I must go and speak to her.' Before Vicky could protest, she had risen and was making for a table in the corner.

'Tea, please,' Thomas told the waitress when she came, 'and crumpets.'

Vicky fiddled with her gloves, drank some tea and stared at a large palm in a brass pot.

'Have an éclair,' Thomas suggested. 'No? Then you can share my crumpets when I get them.'

'I have finished, thank you.'

'You'll have to have one crumpet or I shall feel greedy. Did you know about Alex Beaumont?'

Vicky looked up swiftly, colour running into her cheeks. 'What about him?'

'Jumped his bail and disappeared. Probably gone abroad.'

Vicky stared at him for some minutes while he poured out his tea and began to eat a crumpet with evident pleasure and appetite. At last she said,

'Then he has escaped the law? Will they ever catch him?'

Thomas shrugged. 'If he can get to the Americas, probably not. I suspect someone is helping him, possibly one of his family who wants to be rid of him and hush up the scandal. He'll never be able to return, of course. You know, I feel rather sorry for him, his life won't be much fun from now on.'

'Well he deserved it, he's a criminal.'

'How cruel women are,' he sighed. 'Do have a crumpet, I dislike eating alone.'

She took a crumpet to avoid further argument and for some minutes there was silence. Then she asked,

'Is Effie Grange very much upset?'

'I imagine so, since she's been sent to visit an aunt in Paris where, I hope, she will find enough amusement to drive Alex out of her mind. By the way, have you managed to get over your infatuation for the handsome Alex?'

For a moment she was too indignant to speak. He really was quite insufferable! Through stiff lips she began to say,

'If you are going to be insulting, I shall leave—'

'I'm not. Sorry I had to ask, but I really did have to know. Now, don't you want to know what happened after your flight from the Falconer nursery?'

She hesitated, torn by irritation and curiosity. Curiosity won.

'What *did* happen? Was Lady Falconer terribly angry?'

'Actually, not too furious. After entertaining a houseparty, giving a ball, being involved with a burglary and police swarming all over the place asking questions, and then discovering one of her most popular visitors was a thief—well, you know, I don't think she had energy enough to be further distressed. That girl, Sue, took over and seems to do the work well. Lady Falconer did wonder if you had taken the teaspoons with you, but someone told her you had a dying aunt. You didn't mean Mrs Pendred, did you? I've seldom seen anyone in more splendid health.'

Vicky did not answer him. She was wondering how it was possible to maintain two diametrically opposite wishes. She wished her aunt would return and put an end to this tête-à-tête—and equally strongly hoped she would remain with Lady Oxwell congratulating her on not being dead.

'How are your parents taking it?' Thomas asked abruptly. He was looking at her hard and there was no laughter in his eyes as he went on: 'Are they going to be beastly about things? I expect your mother is still shocked, but your father struck me as a man who could understand. You take after him, I think.'

She nodded. 'Aunt Matilda says I do. They haven't said any more, but I expect there will be something . . .'

'Well, don't run away, that won't solve anything?'

'I have no intention of running away,' she said sharply.

'Splendid. Then you can remain in London and marry me.'

She opened her mouth, then shut it. Words seemed to have failed her just when she most wanted them to convince this impossible man she had not the slightest . . . would never even consider . . .

'Don't say it,' he urged, 'you'll only have to apologise later. Here's your aunt. You know, I think she's one of the nicest aunts I know.'

A sudden idea struck her. 'Did she tell you to meet us here?'

'What a suspicious mind you have. The answer is no. I saw you at the exhibition and followed you.' He got up as

Mrs Pendred approached. 'May I see you to your carriage, Mrs Pendred?'

'Certainly, after I have paid the waitress for our tea.'

'Oh, please allow me.'

'If you insist,' Mrs Pendred said graciously. She had sensible views on saving money when possible.

He saw them to the carriage and waved his top-hat as they drove off. Mrs Pendred arranged her furs and said,

'An excellent young man. If I'd been thirty years younger I would have married him.'

'But not unless he wanted it,' Vicky spoke without thinking and felt her face grow warm. 'Thomas does exactly what *he* likes, not what other people want. He is as obstinate as—as—'

'As a man who has made up his mind about the girl he wants to marry. You will be a fool if you let him go. He'll keep you in order.'

Vicky counted ten slowly, then said: 'I would rather leave Thomas Craig out of our conversation from now on, Aunt Matilda. Did you have a pleasant chat with Lady Oxwell?'

Two days after this, Mrs Pendred announced London air was killing her and society had sadly deteriorated since her day, and she was returning to Norfolk.

Vicky was sorry to see her go, yet felt there might be a better chance of forgetting Thomas and his ridiculous ideas if her aunt was not there to keep reminding her what an excellent husband he would make.

Lady Lynton was extremely relieved, although she made a brave show of hiding it.

'Your mother regards me much as she would an earthquake,' Mrs Pendred remarked to Vicky. 'I upset things, and she thinks me a bad influence on you. She's a good woman and has most nobly done her duty to her husband, although it's a pity she didn't produce a son.'

'Has Mama, or Father, said anything about me to you?' Vicky asked, slightly anxious at what might lie in store once her aunt had ceased to protect her.

'No. They consider I encouraged you to kick over the traces and become Annie Fisher.'

'But you didn't.'

'Of course I didn't. You have quite enough devilment in you without encouragement from anyone.'

'I shall miss you dreadfully,' Vicky said impulsively. 'Thank you for being so kind to me.'

'You needn't thank me. Life in Norfolk can be dull at times. Let me know when you are marrying your duke.'

'Oh—I thought you imagined—'

'Thomas? He hasn't written or called, has he? No, he has changed his mind. You had better begin looking out for someone else.'

Thomas had not called, nor did he call during the next two weeks. They were not particularly pleasant weeks for Vicky. Her father called her into his study and had some blistering comments to make on her behaviour. Having done so, he did not return to the matter, for which she was grateful.

Her mother, on the other hand, continued to refer to her disgraceful deception of her trusting parents, usually tearfully and with an added reproach for having dragged Maud into it.

Vicky was finding life quite extraordinarily flat and dull. She got no news of Wellbury Court, if Sue was coping well with the children, or if Mr Brett had ever solved the mystery of the stolen photograph and plate. And as time went on, there was still no sign of Thomas.

Of course she did not *want* to see him—or did she? Was Aunt Matilda right in thinking he had lost interest and some other girl would grab him? Vicky was astonished at how the idea displeased her! If Thomas had accepted her refusal to listen to his odd notion, he might very well be caught on the rebound. Memories of various young men who had, on being refused by the girl they professed to adore, soon consoled themselves with another choice, kept recurring to her and were both unwelcome and depressing.

She found several reasons for visiting Gunter's, all valid to everyone but herself. She kept a watch on the crowds strolling in the parks on fine mornings and was rewarded by a glimpse of Lady Grange passing in her carriage and a radiant Maud and Archie Burnley on horseback.

She had sent Sue a poste restante address and had received a short note written in purple ink.

'Lady F. was ever so annoyed and I got a proper scolding for not saying something. But I'm head nurse now, just like you said, and there's a girl coming to help next week. Hoping this finds you as it leaves me . . .'

It did not. Sue was contented and happy with her life. Vicky knew she was becoming increasingly restless and dissatisfied with everything and there did not seem much she could do about it. Everyone was busy with their own affairs: Harriet was occupied with her trousseau and Maud spent all possible time with Archie.

If only Thomas would come!

Vicky had never been afraid to face facts, and the fact that she was wishing more and more deeply to see Thomas again had to be faced no matter how much it dismayed her or complicated life.

'I like him,' she thought as she sat in the library window staring out at the wet street and hurrying figures clutching umbrellas. 'I think I have always liked him, even when I thought I hated him. And I never really believed he stole the emeralds . . . And he did save my life that time in the lane.'

She looked up as her father came into the room. He stared at her, frowning, for some moments and she wondered, without much interest, if she was to be scolded again.

'You're looking peaky,' he announced. 'You're pale and drooping. You need a tonic; I'll speak to your mother. What's the matter? A bruised conscience? You needn't bother about what's happened, it's over and done with. Anyway, it wasn't anything disgraceful and we've made too much fuss about it. Matilda was right when she said you were high-spirited and we must expect you to raise the devil sometimes.' He stroked his moustache. 'You're not like the other girls.'

'The last Miss Lynton is a sad disappointment to you, I know, Father.'

'Damn it!' her father exploded. 'I wish your sisters had some of your devilment!' He glanced uneasily at the door. 'But for heaven's sake don't tell your mother I said so.'

Vicky got up and ran to him, suddenly longing for the comfort of his arms as she had when a child and things were going wrong for her.

He held her, peering down into her face. 'What's the matter, child? You're not happy. It isn't that Beaumont fellow?'

'Oh no, Father. I *was* infatuated, I really did think I was falling in love with him—but I know I was wrong.'

'Well thank God for that. Then it's that Craig chap who called the day you came back. He was at Wellbury Court too, wasn't he? And recognised you and didn't give you away. Where is he?'

'I don't know. He's only a—a friend.'

'Pity, I liked the look of him. Clever young fellow, I'm told, and he handled the Beaumont affair well. You know Beaumont skipped his bail?' She nodded. 'Nasty thing, the whole affair. Would you like to go to Italy? Flora is renting a villa there near Naples for three months and—'

'Oh no—I'd rather stay in London.'

'Well we'll see about that tonic. I don't like to see you looking seedy, Vicky.' He kissed her and she slipped from the room, a little comforted. But the knot of unrest was still inside her, slowly tightening as the days passed and Thomas did not come.

The thin winter sunshine tempted her to a walk in the park one morning. She met friends and walked a little way with them but she was not really interested in their conversation and soon left them and set off across the lawns. She wanted to be alone, to try once more to sort out her distressing medley of feelings, to know what she truly wanted. Two chairs were set out by a shrubbery and she sank onto one and was so deeply occupied with her thoughts that she did not realise someone had taken the other chair until Thomas said,

'Shall we talk about the weather? Or would you rather I told you I've been in love with you since that moment you stopped beside Alex and me in Devonshire House? Take your choice.'

For a moment she did not move. She sat looking across the grass to the glitter of a lake while her heart started to beat at a frightening rate and something seemed to explode inside her, letting in golden sunlight to chase away the dark shadows that had haunted her mind. At last she turned to look at him, at the strong, blunt features, determined chin and steady blue eyes holding a light that brought the blood surging into her face.

'I always find discussing the weather horribly boring,' she said, unable to control a little tremor in her voice.

'And the other subject?' His eyes held hers. 'Would you find that boring, Vicky?'

She shook her head, smiling at him and conscious of a great surge of happiness and excitement.

'No.'

He sighed. 'You really have been a little devil, Vicky. Losing your head over poor Alex, deciding you hated me when I tried to talk some sense into you, believing I pinched the Grange necklace, wandering about in a lane with a wild bull—'

'Where you saved my life.'

'Well, perhaps I did, and that puts you under the obligation to marry me without further argument.'

'It would, of course, be the *only* reason for me to marry you,' she said demurely.

'Minx! Be careful, or I may be driven to embrace you in the sight of everyone and probably be arrested by a park-keeper for assaulting you. You know perfectly well how I feel about you, Miss Lynton.'

'No, I don't!' she said indignantly, sitting up, her chin raised as she stared at him. 'You never said a word that could lead me to think you liked me—much less loved me! You spent your time disapproving of me and—'

'Disapproving of you most thoroughly. Playing at being Annie Fisher and getting entangled with a rotter. When I think what you have put me through, I'm not sure you deserve me!'

She gasped, then fell into helpless laughter. 'Thomas you are *quite* hopeless! I cannot think why I like you!'

'Or why you're in love with me?'

She looked at him and knew she must stop pretending. 'Yes, Thomas.'

There came a sudden blaze in his eyes before he took her hand, kissed it lightly, and held it.

'That's all I want,' he said quietly, 'and shall ever want. You've been in my heart—and next to my heart . . .' He slid his hand inside his morning coat and pulled something out.

'The photograph!' she exclaimed. 'It was ..olen.'

'By me. I suppose you thought it was Alex.'

She nodded, dropping her eyes in confusion. 'Did you take the plate too?'

'Yes. I didn't mean to let Brett print another.'

She was silent for some moments. Then she asked: 'Thomas, *is* your mother a helpless invalid? And did Alex know your family well?'

He raised his brows. 'My mother is in splendid health, I'm glad to say, and my family were never keen on Alex. He had to leave college, you know. Did you believe it all, Vicky?'

She shook her head. 'I don't think I did.' She glanced at her watch and rose in dismay. 'It's terribly late, I must go! Why—there's the carriage and Mama waving to me.'

'I shall escort you to her.'

They crossed the lawn and he handed her into the Lynton carriage and stood, top-hat in hand and said,

'I shall give myself the pleasure of calling upon your youngest daughter tomorrow, Lady Lynton.'

Lady Lynton was far too well bred to look back at him as the carriage moved on. She said: 'Vicky—' but one glance at her daughter's face silenced her, and she had to content herself with drawing her ermine stole around her shoulders with bewildered resignation tinged with hope.

Vicky lay back, her face softly flushed and a smile playing around her lips. Her strange and lovely eyes were dreamy and she was not even trying to assess her emotions. It was enough that she was floating on a rosy cloud of happiness. She was remembering how Thomas had looked at her that evening in Devonshire House and how it had seemed of no importance to her then; his coming to the nursery to ask how her ankle was the day she had hurt it. He had said it could be of importance to 'someone' and she had been idiotic enough to think he meant Alex. And he had once said her hair was too pretty to be hidden by a cap . . .

For the rest of the day she moved in a dream. At dinner, Sir Andrew remarked on her improved appearance and put it down to the tonic.

'I shan't be able to sleep a wink,' she thought, but she was lost in dreams of Wellbury Court and Thomas before she knew it. She awoke to see the maid taking a dress out of the wardrobe.

'Not that one,' she said, 'the rose velvet.'

She was in the library when he came. He paused for a second as she turned from the window and faced him, tall and slender in her rose gown, her eyes greenly luminous and her soft lips parted in a smile.

'Vicky!' He had her in his arms, holding her as if he never meant to let her go, and kissing her like a lover who had hungered for her kisses.

She slid her arms around his neck, clinging to him. So this was love, this deep, heart-shaking feeling that took over her whole being. This unacknowledged longing that had been satisfied at last, this blessed release from unrest and uncertainty! This utter abandonment to the man who mattered more than anyone in the world!

He looked down at her. 'You mean it, my dearest one? You'll marry me—soon?'

'But you haven't proposed!' She laughed at him. 'You haven't *asked* me to marry you, only told me I'm going to. It is all very unorthodox.'

'I'm an unorthodox person, and so are you, my wicked, enchanting little nursemaid.' He slid his hand under her chin, tilting her radiant face to his and kissed her softly. 'My beloved darling, you are mine and I shall never let you go!'

'Good God!'

They turned to see Sir Andrew standing staring at them. Before he could say more, Vicky slipped her arm through Thomas's and said gaily,

'You remember Thomas, Father? I'm going to marry him.'

'I certainly hope so, after the way you've been behaving.' Sir Andrew advanced into the room, a faint twinkle underlying the sternness of his eyes. 'And why have I not been told about this?'

'I've only just realised I want to marry him,' his daughter told him happily. 'You will give us your blessing, won't you, Father?'

'I don't suppose it would do much good if I didn't, you'd dash off and become a cook or something.'

'I will take good care of her, sir,' Thomas said, meeting Sir Andrew's searching glance.

'I'm glad to hear it. I suppose this is why you have been looking like that girl in the picture called "The Deserted Maiden", Vicky.'

'Yes,' she agreed, 'I thought Thomas had deserted me, but he hasn't, and I love him and we would like to get married quite soon, please.'

Sir Andrew groaned dramatically. 'Harriet, Maud and now you! I shall be ruined. Come and kiss me, child—and tell that young man of yours he hasn't at all done the proper thing, he should have asked me if I would allow you to permit his attentions.'

Thomas grinned cheerfully. 'Since she *has* allowed them, sir, it is only for me to ask if I may have the very great honour of marrying your youngest daughter.'

Sir Andrew waved the copy of *The Times* he held. 'Take her, my boy. She's my last and—' he shot a quick look at the door and lowered his voice, '—and the best.'

Thomas, his eyes on Vicky's smiling face, murmured: 'The last and best and most beautiful and my heart's dearest darling!'

'Nicely put,' Sir Andrew said approvingly. 'Run and find your mother, Vicky, and give me time to find if Thomas can support you without your having to go out as a nurse or washerwoman, then bring her down to meet her future son-in-law. And tell someone to see there's champagne for lunch.'